Lassa Hope ar ... man

by

Emma Charlish

Chapter One

Introducing Lassa

Lassa Hope declined the last cookie on the plate with a shake of her head. She had already

eaten nine. One more and she would surely pop. Her mouth was so full of the heavenly

sweet doughy mixture that she could barely keep it closed as she chewed. 'All things in

moderation' was a phrase lost on Lassa.

Lassa lived with her paternal grandparents in a first floor council flat in Staffordshire. Her parents had died in a car collision when she was just sixteen months old. Neither her mother

nor her father had been wearing a seat belt and as a result they had both died on impact.

Lassa, however, had been safely secured in the rear of the vehicle and had been lucky to

survive without a scratch.

She had just celebrated her thirteenth birthday. A plump, pretty girl with shoulder length

auburn hair and a face full of freckles she despised, she spent much of her time listening to

the latest pop music on her grandfather's age-old music system, or reading Jacqueline Wilson

books in her bedroom. Although of an amiable and chirpy disposition, Lassa preferred her

own company. She rarely met up with classmates after school and did not attend evening youth clubs or other recreational groups that proved popular with her peers. As a

consequence, Lassa had very few friends.

Lassa was a solitary child due largely to her own self-loathing. She was a good nine

pounds overweight and it made her feel utterly miserable, in the most part due to the cruel

name-calling to which she was subjected on a daily basis. And yet as the pounds began to

creep on with the onset of puberty, her desire to eat chocolate, cakes and other sweet treats

never waned. She loved roast dinners too, with soft Yorkshire puddings and oodles of thick,

delicious gravy. And she couldn't get enough of her grandmother's apple crumble and

dreamy Devon custard. Heaven for Lassa meant eating fish, chips and mushy peas until

her plate was licked clean or until she felt physically sick, whichever happened soonest.

"Oh go on, have it," her grandmother urged her kindly, waving the plate in front of her

face. "One more won't kill you."

The very moment Lassa had rejected the last remaining cookie, it had seemed to cry out to

her, silently willing her to reach out and grab it with both hands, to cram it greedily into her

mouth and to devour it. Lassa was finding it hard to resist. Her resolve was weak. And now

her grandmother was putting pressure on for her to consume it too. She knew she was

fighting a losing battle.

Lassa regarded the rolls of puppy fat around her middle with disdain.

"Nan, I shouldn't," she said unconvincingly. "Really I shouldn't."

Her grandmother picked up the cookie from the plate and passed it to her.

"Nonsense!" she said. "Go on, you know you want to."

Over in the far corner of the room, Ernest Hope shuffled in his armchair and reached for the television remote control resting on the nest of Mahogany coffee tables beside him.

"Nance, leave the poor girl alone," he admonished his wife gently. "Can't you hear what she's telling you? She doesn't want the blasted thing."

He pointed the remote control at the television and punched at the volume control, plunging the room into silence.

He was a tall, thin man in his early seventies, pale and gaunt and no longer in the best of health due to an arthritic hip that plagued him constantly, and which had left him virtually housebound for years.

"Besides," he said with a wink in Lassa's direction. "I want it."

Nance chuckled. "And I suppose you'll be wanting a nice cup of tea to wash it down

with?" she asked with a smile.

She passed him the last cookie and walked into the kitchen without waiting for his

response. She knew Ern would never refuse a hot cup of tea. Milk with two sugars, that's

how he liked it. After nearly fifty years of marriage, there was nothing Ern and Nance didn't

know about the other.

"How are things, Lassa?" Ern asked his granddaughter when he knew they were alone and

out of earshot. His brow was furrowed in concern. After finding Lassa in her bedroom one

evening, crying into her hands, she had confided in him, albeit reluctantly, about the group of

girls in her tutor group that were giving her a hard time; name-calling mostly, but occasionally giving her the odd slap or two. His heart had broken into a thousand pieces that

day as he had listened to her, her body racked with sobs as she spoke. He had never felt so

old and useless.

Lassa suddenly felt uncomfortable and her face turned pink with shame. She hadn't liked

to worry her grandfather, but it had felt good to have finally had someone to confide in.

"Things are getting better, Pops," she replied, feigning a smile. She had called him 'Pops'

for as long as she could remember. "I hardly ever see Clare Fox these days."

Lassa was lying and Ern knew it. He was not so easy to fool. But he chose to drop the

subject for now.

"Have you done your homework?" he asked. He punched at the remote control again and the room instantly filled with the sounds of a gunfight in a black and white western movie.

"That project of yours needs to be handed in soon, doesn't it?"

Lassa heaved a sigh of relief, more comfortable with this line of conversation.

"All done," she said.

In fact, she'd enjoyed working on the project on the Industrial Revolution so much she

had exceeded the minimum word length by five hundred. The teacher had said the class

could work in pairs if they had wanted to, but nobody had seemed keen to double up with

Lassa, and so she had worked alone.

"I'm going to pack my rucksack ready for school tomorrow," Lassa said suddenly, rising

up from her position on the sofa. "Then I think I'll read in bed for a bit before calling it a night. I'm really tired."

Lassa called '<u>Goodnight</u>' to her grandmother and blew her grandfather a kiss before

walking out of the living room and into her bedroom, which was located directly across the

hall. With its floral patterned wallpaper, royal blue carpet and walnut furniture, it was by no

means upbeat or contemporary. But it was comfortable and clean, warm and safe, and that

was all that mattered to Lassa. She had personalised it with posters of her favourite actors

and pop stars. Numerous pictures of Justin Bieber smiled at her from the walls, and a popular

boy band – naked to the waist – stared moodily down at her from the ceiling above the bed

where she slept. Shelves attached to the wall were packed to each end with Jaqueline Wilson books, other fiction paperbacks and dictionaries. And fluffy pink scatter cushions were

strewn all about; on the floor, on the bed and on the ottoman that stretched out beneath the

window sill.

Lassa packed her school rucksack with the text books she required for the next day's

lessons. She was not looking forward to going back to school. She had found herself living

for the weekends, but they always seemed to pass by so quickly. Lassa knew she was

wishing her life away, but she couldn't wait for the day when she would be old enough never

to have to walk through the school gates again.

It wasn't the lessons that she loathed so much, nor was it the school dinners, although they

were only marginally edible. No, she hated school because of one group of three girls in her tutor group: Clare Fox and her friends, Sam Burdekin and Michelle Burke.

Clare was the leader of the group, an obnoxious fourteen year old with an utter contempt

for anyone's feelings other than her own. She was tall for her age, with long, dark, unkempt

hair that she usually wore scraped back into a high ponytail to expose a forehead speckled

with masses of tiny spots, red and angry looking. Greasy and thick, the single tress

descended the length of her back like a rat's tail. Her teeth were bucked and stained yellow

and her ears stuck out like the wing nuts on a chair frame.

And yet despite her own obvious shortcomings, Clare Fox made Lassa's life a misery,

regularly taunting her about her size, her freckles and the colour of her hair. She had

knocked Lassa to the ground once, stealing her dinner money, and had spat at her on more than one occasion.

In short, Clare Fox was a bully.

Lassa removed her clothes and dressed herself in a pair of light-weight, blue cotton

pyjamas. Then she went into the bathroom, where she washed, brushed her teeth and flossed,

before returning to her bedroom to retire for the night.

Lassa picked up her book from the nightstand: Four Children and It, Jacqueline Wilson's

contemporary version of Lassa's favourite story by E Nesbit, and began to read. All too

soon, however, she became distracted with thoughts of school and she began to weep quietly.

She made a silent prayer that tomorrow Clare Fox would leave her alone. It was a prayer that

she made every school night.

And one that was very rarely answered.

*

The walk to school for Lassa was a long one, a good two and a half miles as the crow flies,

but choosing not to walk would mean her having to catch two different buses. And Clare Fox

and her gang usually travelled to school by bus, so that just wasn't an option.

There were closer schools of course, but Gibbet Hill Secondary School and Community

College had an excellent reputation, having consistently been placed in the top 20 in the

national league table for academic achievement.

Ern and Nance had been over the moon when Lassa had been accepted there, since the amount of places offered to students residing outside of its catchment area were in single

figures.

Gibbet Hill Secondary School and Community College was built in 1975 and catered for a

thousand students of 11-18 years of age. It boasted five science laboratories, a music suite

with rehearsal rooms, a Home Economics and Textiles area and a Design and Technology

Centre. The school was housed in modern buildings and included exceptional facilities,

such as a sports hall, an all-weather sports pitch, an indoor swimming pool, an Extended

Resources Centre and a Humanities wing.

As its name suggested, it was erected on the site where highwaymen and other felons were

gibbeted in the 18th Century. The last man to be gibbeted there was a Moses Menzies, who was put to his death outside Newgate Prison in 1765. It was reported that three thousand

people attended his execution on that cold winter's day. Many had brought their lunch and a

stool to make a real occasion of it.

Menzies' last recorded words to the overseeing Alderman were to acknowledge his

sentence and to freely forgive those who had been instrumental in convicting him, although

he maintained his innocence right until the very end, just as he had at his trial.

It was a particularly gruesome and unusual execution. Once the ladder had been kicked

away and Menzies was declared dead, his lifeless body was then treated with a tar coating

and enclosed within a close-fitting harness of chains and steel. His corpse was then taken to

be hung on the gibbet in the place of his arrest, his home town, and there his skeleton remained on show until 1805, some forty years later.

Legend had it that on the anniversary of his death, the spirit of Menzies would return to

wander the school grounds. Indeed, many locals had claimed to have heard him weeping

softly, pleading his innocence from beyond the grave.

Not that Lassa believed in all that mumbo jumbo. She was a complete sceptic and refused

to attribute strange sightings or odd occurrences to the supernatural; she merely consigned

them to that portion of her brain she had labelled 'The Unexplained'. She was certain that

there was a logical explanation for all things weird and wonderful; scientists were just yet to

find it. Albert Einstein theorised the possibility of a multi-dimensional reality, saying that

ghosts were merely echoes from the past, resurfacing in our time when the relative dimensions met. That was all far too high-brow for Lassa, however, so she decided not to

dwell on the matter of ghosts, spectres and phantoms or whatever else the undead might be

called.

Lassa was just five minutes from the school gates when she rounded the corner into Bott

Lane. But the sight that greeted her was the one that she feared the most. A knot of dread

tightened in her stomach and her heart began to thud against her ribcage. There, standing in

front of Sagoo's Grocery Store, stood Clare Fox, chewing gum, kicking her heels and

laughing with Sam Burdekin and Michelle Burke, her mindlessly faithful cronies. As she

neared, Lassa took a deep breath and clutched her rucksack closer to her chest. She felt her

throat turn dry and her legs turn to jelly.

"Well look who it is," Clare declared in a sing-song voice as Lassa approached. "It's Lardy No-Hope." She turned to Sam and Michelle with a sneer. "She's so big her school photos have to be taken with a wide lens."

Sam and Michelle laughed on cue, just as Clare would have expected them to. Clare walked slowly and deliberately in front of Lassa to block her path. Sam and Michelle closed in, one on either side of her, their breath hot on her face.

"Turn out your pockets then, No-Hope," Clare said gruffly. "Let's see what you've got for us today."

Lassa swallowed hard and locked her trembling knees together to keep herself on her feet.

"I haven't got anything," she protested weakly.

Clare stood before her and lifted Lassa's face upwards.

"Don't lie to me, you fat cow!" she snarled. At her sides, Sam and Michelle sniggered.

Lassa tried to glance at them, but Clare's fingers on chin prevented her from moving her

head. "You've always got something. Even if it's a slice of your grandma's rotten

homemade banana cake."

What little colour remained in Lassa's face drained away.

"It's true, honest," she said lamely. "I've got nothing you'd want."

Clare released her grip and allowed her arms to fall to her sides. Her face was thunderous.

"I think you're lying," she spat, glaring at her.

Lassa massaged her bruised chin.

"I'm not," she whimpered. She felt hot tears pricking at the back of her eyes, but she

refused to cry.

Clare grabbed a hold of Lassa's right arm and twisted it savagely.

Lassa let out a gasp and sank to her knees. Her rucksack fell to the floor. Whilst Sam and

Michelle rifled through it, Clare moved behind her, holding her arm straight back, still

twisting hard. The pain in Lassa's shoulder was tremendous from the torque of the grip and

she let out a scream of anguish. Her cheeks were now wet with tears.

"Hey! I've found her homework!" cried Michelle, holding it aloft triumphantly. She

kicked the rucksack away from her and began to click through the leaves of the project. "It's

all neat and nerdy; there's loads of pictures and writing. What a geek!"

Clare's steely blue eyes flashed. She snatched the project away from Michelle's hands,

regarded it briefly, then threw it into the kerb. The pages scattered and proceeded to blow up the street in the wind.

"No good to us though, is it?" she declared huffily.

Lassa rose unsteadily to her feet to retrieve her rucksack and the remainder of its contents.

"It took me ages to do that," she said gravely.

"More fool you, teacher's pet," Clare replied nastily. "Maybe next time you'll be sure to

have something we actually want." She seized a length of Lassa's hair and tugged it down to

waist level, holding it there as she spoke. "Do you understand?"

Shockwaves of pain spiralled from Lassa's scalp down through the right side of her body.

She howled out in agony.

"Let go! Please let go!" she pleaded.

Suddenly Mr Sagoo appeared at the threshold of his grocery store, having heard the commotion from inside. His face was red with anger.

"Stop that! Stop that at once!" he yelled, his eyes blazing. "Leave that poor girl alone!"

Clare released her hold on Lassa and turned to face Mr Sagoo in disgust.

"What's it to do with you?" she asked him rudely.

Mr Sagoo advanced towards her menacingly.

Lassa, realising that this was the diversion she needed to escape, collected her things

together and with a sudden but welcome burst of adrenaline, began to run as fast as she could

towards the school. Within moments, Clare, Sam and Michelle were hot on her heels,

hollering and screaming like banshees.

Lassa bolted up Bott Lane like a Grand National winner, leaving the three angry girls

trailing in her wake. She did not know where she had acquired her energy from, but she was grateful for it.

Reaching the end of the lane, she proceeded to run up the dirt track that led directly to the

back of the school. She continued to run so fast and so hard that she left imprints in the soft

earth on the ground. Her heart was pounding and her legs were tiring. But the bullies' legs

were tiring also and they had fallen far behind. Lassa knew this did not give cause for her to

slow down, but she also knew that she could not maintain her current speed.

Before too long she came across a large Elm tree. She had probably passed it a hundred

times before, but not until now had she really noticed it, though it was at least twenty metres

tall and five metres in girth. The strongest of its branches appeared to extend a fair distance up the trunk. Lassa knew what she must do. With one powerful leap, she caught the lowest

branch and swung herself up among the leaves. Surprising herself, she climbed quickly,

pushed on by sheer panic, feeling the tree quake beneath her grappling hands and feet. She

cradled herself in between three intertwining branches and waited, holding her breath, her

chest rising and falling painfully.

Presently Clare, Sam and Michelle reached the tree. They were walking now, their

breathing laboured.

"I swear I'm gonna have that fat cow when I see her next," Lassa heard Clare say. "She's

got it coming to her, mark my words."

She saw Sam soberly nod her head in agreement.

"Did you see her face when her homework went flying up the street?" Michelle tittered.

She was a good head shorter than Clare with cropped black hair, much like a boy's. Her

school blouse was wrinkled and grubby-looking and she looked as though she hadn't had a

good wash in weeks. "I thought she was going to start blubbing!"

"She's going to wish she'd never been born," Clare assured her friends ominously.

When the three girls passed by, Lassa began to rhythmically bang her head against the

tree branch in front of her. Frustrated with herself for her cowardice, and with a throat raw

from trying to hold back the sobs that welled within her chest to occasionally escape as a

single, brief mewling sound, she found herself wishing she could just run away and never

come back. But her grandparents had already lost their son and daughter-in-law, to lose their

granddaughter too would surely devastate them. Lassa could never bring herself to do it.

Lassa remained in the tree for a few minutes more, smelling the leaves and breathing the fresh, free air before reluctantly beginning the climb downward.

The remainder of her journey was thankfully uneventful but as she ambled through the school gates, tears leaked uncontrollably from her eyes. She knew that her tormentors would be waiting.

As luck would have it, Lassa was not late for school. Conversely, Clare, Sam and Michelle were. Heaven only knew where they had been or what they had been up to, since they had been ahead of Lassa at one point and should have arrived before her. And yet they sauntered into the form room at just after 9:15, missing the call of the register, but in time to hear the bell that signalled the start of the first period. Biology was the first lesson of the day.

With the bell still ringing in their ears, the tutor group piled out of the room and down the

corridor towards the science block, chatting easily with each other about how they had spent

their weekends. All except Lassa that is; she sloped disconsolately behind, still mulling over

that morning's events. Fortunately the form tutor had detained Clare, Sam and Michelle to

speak to them about their late appearance. They would now most certainly be referred to

Mr Haughton, the Head of Year, to explain the reason behind their unpunctuality. The upshot

of that would mean that they would not be able to attend first period, therefore giving Lassa

an hour's respite. But Lassa knew that this would only serve to delay the inevitable. They

would catch up with her sooner or later.

Biology was Lassa's favourite lesson, but it was marred by the lingering feeling of dread lodged in the back of her throat like a greased rag. Her stomach was in knots. She felt

frightened and isolated, but above all ashamed for being such an easy victim. She wished she

could be stronger, more assertive, like Marvel's The Black Widow, but she just didn't have it

in her to be a superhero. She imagined her grandparents would be disappointed beyond

measure if they knew just how weak she was. She had spoken to Pops about it, of course, but

even he didn't know the half of it.

Before long the lesson was over and she and her fellow students were vacating the

room. As she had expected, Clare, Sam and Michelle were waiting for her outside, their

anger at her fuelled further still by the severe dressing down they had received from

Mr Haughton.

Clare spotted Lassa immediately and approached her slowly, fury written all over her spotty face. She nodded to Sam and Michelle, who obediently took their places at either end

of the small corridor, plainly on the lookout for teachers.

Lassa looked forlornly down at her feet and her whole body tensed with a sense of

expectancy.

"Thought you'd get away from me, did you, Lardy?" Clare asked vehemently. "Did you

really think you would get the better of me?" She gritted her yellow teeth and edged closer,

her fists balled at hers sides. "Just who do you think you are?" she hissed.

Lassa raised her head and regarded Clare with wide-open, frightened eyes.

"I'm a nobody," she said flatly.

Clare wrapped a hand around Lassa's throat.

"I'm gonna teach you a lesson you'll never forget, No-Hope," she said icily, her dark blue

eyes narrowed to slits.

Lassa struggled to focus through the tears that had begun to well in her eyes. She could

sense her knees buckling beneath her and she felt dizzy suddenly, aware only of Clare's grip

about her neck.

"I'm gonna make you wish you'd died in that car crash along with your mum and dad,"

Clare warned nastily, tightening her grip.

Lassa closed her eyes.

The waiting was finally over.

*

Chapter Two

Introducing Philomena

Professor Philomena Dovetail donned her protective Perspex eye goggles and took a precautionary step backwards. On the wooden desk before her, the flame of a Bunsen

Burner began to lick about the crescent-shaped bottom of a glass test tube with unwavering

exactness, swiftly heating its red liquid contents to the boiling point. The high temperature

worked as a catalyst to produce a change in colour: From red to blue, blue to green, green to

yellow. All the shades of the rainbow were eventually represented, one after the other in

hasty succession, as the liquid bubbled away busily in its slim glass container. This was an

identical reaction to the one the Professor had anticipated and she could not have been more

delighted. She threw up her hands in elation.

"Buckles and bootlaces!" she cried. "I've done it at last!"

But then the bubbling became more urgent and the frothing liquid began to push up, spilling out over the brim like an erupting volcano, pouring onto the wooden desk and

burning a hole right through it to land in a technicolour puddle on the floor. The tripod, to

which the test tube was secured, began to tremble with the power and velocity of the

eruption, rattling noisily on the desk like an unsettled baby shaking the bars of its

cot, until it lost its balance and tumbled to the concrete floor.

The professor sighed with disappointment and shook her head wearily as she removed her

goggles and slung them onto the desk, scattering wire gauze, spatulas and other scientific

paraphernalia across its vast wooden length.

As someone who loved change, but who hated decorating, Philomena had embarked some

time ago upon a quest to invent an ever-changing emulsion paint, which she had dubbed The

Chameleon. She had hoped to patent the idea of The Chameleon, market the product and make her fortune. However, whilst she had experienced some early successes, she was yet to find the final formula.

She had hoped the paint would have chameleon-like properties, hence the working title, automatically changing colour to blend in with the most dominant colour in a room, so that if ever a new suite, carpet or curtains was introduced, the surrounding walls would transform accordingly to match. The aim was for homeowners and tenants never to have to go to the expense and effort of decorating more than once in their lifetime.

In the staff room her colleagues had trivialised her ideas as being “pie in the sky”, poo-

pooing them as not being viable. Nevertheless Philomena was determined to make a name

for herself, to be recognised internationally for services rendered by her amazing discoveries

and investigations, and to eventually be granted The Nobel Prize for intellectual

achievements in Chemistry.

Despite numerous knock-backs and a distinct lack of encouragement, support and interest,

Philomena was not prepared to give up on her dream just yet.

She was an eccentric fifty-eight year old woman of Bohemian tastes. Born in Paris, France

to a Pakistani mother and a British father, she was fluent in six languages, one of which was

no longer spoken in the Modern World. She was the Head of Science (incorporating

Chemistry, Physics and Biology) at Gibbet Hill Secondary School and Community College, where she had worked for the past seventeen years. She was popular with the students,

largely for her laid-back Come What May attitude to life, and also with the staff, due to her

excellent home-brewed beer and cherry tomato wine (the former for which Mr Bergin, the

Head of Physical Education, said she deserved the Nobel Prize alone).

Scatty, clumsy, but certainly unique, Philomena sported an unruly mop of grey-white hair

and possessed wild dark eyes that seemed to bore right into your very soul. Her caramel-

coloured face was made up of an avalanche of wrinkles and was peppered with premature

liver spots. However, though age had evidently taken its toll, she remained a very attractive

woman.

Her dress sense was non-conventional for the age. As a rule she favoured loose fitting, flowing garments of brilliant colours and atypical fabrics and open-toed leather sandals that

would have been more at home in the Roman Empire.

Avant-garde jewellery decorated her slender wrists, neck and fingers, and a large, freshly

cut flower could always be found adorning her hair.

Without a doubt, Professor Philomena Dovetail could by no means be described as

ordinary.

Suddenly the silence was broken by the sound of a scuffle. Angry voices and loud

crashes resounded through the room. Philomena jumped in surprise.

"What is that hullabaloo?" Philomena remarked to herself under her breath.

She walked over to the window and peered through a slit in the Venetian blind. She observed the school playing field. It was empty except for sweet wrappers, chocolate foils

and crisp packets blowing around and around in the wind like a colourful carousel.

Philomena shrugged her shoulders and moved away from the window.

"Humph!" she said to herself, shaking her head.

But then she heard the disturbance again, only louder this time and emanating not from the

playing field as she had first thought, but from outside in the corridor.

She darted to the door and brusquely pulled it open.

"What's all this fuss about?" she demanded to know, her face etched with irritation.

She thought she caught sight of Clare Fox and two other girls, possibly Sam Burdekin and

Michelle Burke - the three were usually joined at the hip – charging through the swing doors at the far end of the corridor and out onto the playing field. It was hard to tell without her

spectacles. She had neglected to replace them after removing them to put on her lab goggles

earlier, and she struggled to see clearly at a distance without them.

There was evidence of a rumpus having taken place. Several books lay open on the

floor, apparently having fallen from their shelving, and pinned to the wall a map of the world

that had previously been intact was now badly torn and lapping down from its top right hand

corner.

Almost at once Philomena saw Lassa, sitting halfway down the empty corridor between a

book cabinet and a wall mounted fire hose reel. She was cradling her knees, her head bowed

low and she was rocking back and forth, sobbing gently.

Philomena approached her slowly, not wanting to alarm her.

"You're Lassa Hope aren't you?" she asked softly as she neared.

Lassa looked up, startled. Her face was red and blotchy from tears. Philomena's heart

went out to her immediately.

"Yes," replied Lassa in a whisper.

Philomena crouched down on her haunches in front of Lassa and held her gaze evenly.

"Do you want to tell me what happened, Lassa?" she asked delicately.

Lassa shook her head and dried her eyes with the sleeve of her blazer.

"No," she sniffed. She drew her knees closer to her chest. "I'm okay, Professor, honest I

am."

But then she started to cry again, great gulping sobs that shook her whole body. Through hiccoughing breaths, she tried to reassure Philomena that she was just being over-sensitive

and silly.

Philomena reached out and stroked Lassa's wet auburn hair away from her tear-stained

face.

"Are you being bullied, Lassa?" she asked solemnly. "Is Clare Fox bullying you?" she

asked more pointedly.

With an impulsive shuddering breath Lassa fell into Philomena and she clung to her,

burying her head in her shoulder, wetting her neck with tears that fell unchecked.

"They don't leave me alone," she cried. "They hate me."

Philomena curled her arms about her and pulled her closer, patting her back in comfort.

She was just about to open her mouth to speak when there was a movement from her right and two Year Eight boys stampeded into the corridor, laughing raucously.

Philomena glanced over her shoulder and threw the boys an irritated look.

"Out!" she said sternly, her voice raised to a level that commanded immediate deference.

The boys turned on their heels quickly and without argument.

Philomena turned back to Lassa. "Let's go inside my lab."

Philomena helped Lassa to her feet and motioned her into the laboratory. She did not have

another lesson planned until after lunch, so she knew they would not be disturbed for at least

another hour. Lassa would be missed, of course: She would be expected in the music suite

for her second lesson of the day, but Philomena would explain her absence to Mr Bosworth in

the staff room later. The matter in hand was far more pressing and she needed to attend to it without delay.

"Sit down," she instructed Lassa, gesturing towards one of the wooden chairs at the front

end of the room. She pulled up a chair next to her and rotated it clockwise so that it faced

her. She took Lassa's hand in her own and waited, silently, allowing her the time she needed

to compose herself. Although her breathing had now calmed and her tears had dried to leave

salt tracks in their place, Lassa was still not ready to talk.

"Now, are you going to tell me exactly what's been going on?" Philomena asked.

Lassa took a deep breath and swallowed hard before finally speaking.

"They call me Lardy No-Hope," she said, and her bottom lip quivered. "They think it's

funny." She looked away, embarrassed. "They hit me too sometimes," she added desolately.

"And spit at me if I refuse to hand over my dinner money. I've never done anything to them.

I can't even remember how or when it all started." She gave a ragged sigh. "But it feels like

it's been going on forever."

"Just to be clear, are you talking about Clare Fox and her friends?" It would come as no

surprise to Philomena. Clare was always getting herself into trouble. She had been

suspended from lessons for two days earlier in the term for starting a food fight in the school

canteen and had arrived at Gibbet Hill Secondary School having been expelled from

another comprehensive three miles away. "Are they the girls that have been bullying you?"

Lassa nodded her head in silent affirmation.

"This stops now, Lassa," Philomena said emphatically, squeezing her hand in reassurance.

"You are no longer alone. This is a problem for the school and it must be tackled. You

should not be made to suffer in this way. School should be a safe haven, a place of learning.

I will speak to Mr Haughton this afternoon; he may say we'll need to get the headmaster

involved – "

"No!" Lassa looked panic stricken. "No, don't," she implored. "Please, Professor.

They'll be excluded from school, but they won't be excluded from my estate. The problem

won't go away. It will only make things worse. They will wait for me after school."

"Do you trust me, Lassa?" Philomena asked her.

"Yes," replied Lassa. And she knew that she did.

"Then leave this with me," Philomena said decisively.

Lassa nodded.

Philomena got to her feet and retrieved her spectacles from her desk. She popped them on

and immediately they slid halfway down her nose. Peering over the tops, she said, "You

know you can talk to me anytime you want to, don't you? My door is always open."

"Thank you," Lassa said shyly. She blushed a little and smiled. A real smile, albeit small

and tremulous.

Philomena gave her a soft pat on the shoulder and smiled back, a flash of white in her

coffee coloured skin.

"You're welcome, Lassa," she said warmly.

Just then, and without warning, the room became icy cold, dropping instantaneously in temperature by twenty degrees or more. Simultaneously a wintry mist began to rise

unhurriedly from a hole in the floor beneath the desk, where one would have expected to see

just concrete. Gradually it began to cloud the room with a thick, ethereal blanket.

The hole was vast, approximately one metre in diameter, and through the haze, it appeared

to be a constructed of a series of small semi-translucent cubes to look like nothing either

Lassa or the Professor had ever seen before.

"Professor – " Lassa's words drifted off. "Professor, what's that?"

Lassa pointed under the desk, her eyes unblinking.

Philomena shook her head in amazement. "I – I don't – I don't know," she mused quietly,

tilting her head for a better look. She drew the narrow lines of her brows together in bewilderment. "I. Really. Don't. Know."

Just then a tiny wren emerged, flying up from the hole through the murkiness to flutter

indiscriminately around the lab. Philomena lurched back in alarm, throwing herself

momentarily off balance. She gripped onto the edge of the desk to steady herself, her eyes

still fixated on the bird.

"Buckles and bootlaces!" she exclaimed. "That bird appeared from the ground!"

The mist continued to pervade the room. Visibility was poor. She and Lassa looked at

each other aghast.

"What's happening?" Lassa rose from her seat and edged cautiously nearer to the core of

the phenomena. "I can hear noises," she said. "It sounds like birds singing – "

There was a loud thud from behind. Lassa and Philomena turned around sharply. The bird had flown into a window, knocking itself out, and was now lying motionless on the lab

counter.

Philomena walked over to it and cupped it carefully in her hands.

"He's alive," she breathed. "He's just a little stunned." She brought him over to Lassa,

who stroked its wing gently. "Let's put him back."

"Put him back where?" Lassa asked her uncertainly, passing a fleeting glance at the hole.

The rising of the mist was now beginning to subside and the room was starting to clear.

"You don't mean to put him back in there, do you?" she said incredulously.

Philomena gazed down at the bird, which was now trembling in the palm of her hand.

"His eyes are opening, he's waking," she said in a low voice. "Let's put him back, yes?

To where he came from?" She looked at Lassa for approval. "He must be lost and scared."

"But we don't know what's in there," Lassa reminded her.

Philomena gave Lassa's words some thought. Finally she said, "I think he needs to return

to his family." She stroked the wren again, running her finger down the middle of its shiny

warm back. "Wouldn't you want to return to your family if you were lost?"

Lassa was not convinced that freeing the bird back into the unknown was such a good idea,

but she felt that by doing this she could learn more about the odd-looking hole; what it was,

where it led to. And so it was her curiosity that ultimately prompted her to concede to

Philomena's appeal.

"All right," she relented finally.

Philomena knelt down beside the hole and released the bird directly over it. It vanished immediately, the opening seeming to swallow it whole. The diaphanous surface trembled

momentarily, reacting to the disturbance, but otherwise it remained constant.

Lassa did not know what she had expected to see, but this had surpassed her wildest

expectations. There seemed to be no rational explanation for what had just occurred. Quite

simply, she was stumped. And yet she had never felt so excited in all her life. Butterflies

danced in the pit of her stomach and her heart raced as though she had been sprinting.

"Professor, I just don't understand any of this," she said unnecessarily. "What does this all

mean – the mist – the bird – the hole -?"

Philomena called to mind the test she had conducted earlier that morning and the unforeseen chemical reaction that had resulted. She remembered how the molecules in the

solution had collided with such force that it had culminated with a pool of what she could

only describe as a puce coloured gloop on the floor. Had her experiment really opened a

portal into an alternate world? Had she inadvertently created a gateway into another

dimension? The very suggestion was inconceivable, preposterous even. But, then, what

was this that she was looking into? Philomena was bamboozled.

"Your guess is as good as mine, Lassa," she said, scratching her head. She told her of her

experiment earlier. "Surely this – this – whatever it is – couldn't have occurred as a result of

that?"

Lassa shifted her body closer to Philomena's.

"Shall we find out?" she asked breathlessly. There was a flush to her face, and when

she spoke her voice quivered with excitement. "If a bird can come through a hole in the

ground – and go back in again – who is to say that we can't?"

Philomena recalled the young girl she had found in the corridor not so long ago, her spirit

broken by bullies. She did not recognise this auburn haired little girl at her side now, full of

exuberant anticipation, as being one and the same.

"Oh Lassa, I don't know – " she began doubtfully.

"Oh please, Professor. PLEASE!" Lassa's last word stretched out for an eternity.

Philomena's face broke into a tremulous smile.

"Okay," she said finally, but not with trepidation. She regretted it instantly, the full impact

of her decision to investigate the hole hitting her like a lightning bolt. She could not shake off a strange feeling of dread and foreboding. She swallowed hard. "But we must be

careful."

Lassa poked tentatively at the shimmering surface of the hole, deeming it to have the

texture of the skin on a thick set custard. Prodding it firmly, it yielded at once to her touch
and her finger broke through to disappear from sight.

At her side Philomena sat on her knees, waiting with bated breath. She was wringing her

hands together in fever anticipation, her lips dry and cracked with a combination of

excitement and angst.

"Be careful, Lassa," she cautioned again.

Lassa withdrew her finger and rubbed at it with her thumb, examining it closely.

"Well whatever it is, it hasn't affected my skin at all. It's still perfectly normal."

Philomena dipped her head, inclining it over the opening of the hole so that her right ear

almost made contact with it.

"Do you hear that?" she asked guardedly, one brow raised querulously. "It sounds like

horses galloping – "

"And the wind blowing - and the birds singing - and leaves rustling in the trees – " Lassa

interrupted. "There's a whole other world down there!" she trilled.

She was enjoying herself so much that she had forgotten all about Clare Fox and her

loathsome friends. Tears and sobs had long since turned to insurmountable gladness. She

was at the threshold of an amazing adventure and a sense of exhilaration was soaring through

her veins like a runaway train.

"I'm going to put my arm in," she said, practically panting in excitement. And, without further ado, and oblivious to Philomena's discouraging expression, she plunged her entire arm into the hole and groped around in the unknown. "I feel something!" she cried out just a few moments later.

She pressed her palm against something firm and soft and moist, about a metre south of the hole. She picked at it and when she pulled out her arm she found between her fingers a sod of dewy fresh grass about two inches square. Tiny flecks of dirt clung to her skin. She thought her eyes must be deceiving her.

"It's grass!" she marvelled. "Real grass. But how - ?" Her voice hitched and broke, sliding through the octaves in astonishment. She took a deep breath. "I have to go in!" she decided at once.

Philomena was paralysed with a hurricane of mixed emotions. "I don't think that's a very

good idea, Lassa." She gave a nervous little laugh. "We have no idea what this is or what it

could – "

But it was too late. Lassa had already launched herself head first through the opening,

leaving only her legs visible in the lab to rise at a rigid acute angle from the concrete floor.

Philomena promptly grabbed a hold of them by the ankles and yelled out. "Lassa!

Lassa!" The panic in her voice was palpable. "Lassa!"

But Lassa did not reply.

*

Chapter Three

1765

Lassa could not believe her eyes.

She was now propped up by her elbows on what appeared to be a deserted area of heath

land. Strong and unbending they supported the upper part of her body, whilst behind her, her

legs were no longer discernible. She had not yet pulled them through the void and so they

appeared to be cut off at the thighs, though she could still feel them and would wiggle them,

if only the Professor would loosen the grip on her ankles. Philomena was clutching on to

them so tightly, Lassa feared that the circulation of blood around her body would be impeded.

Summoning all of her strength, Lassa heaved herself forward, hauling her legs free of

Philomena's grasp with one fluid movement. She leapt to her feet and observed the space

behind her. Just one foot from the ground there appeared to a circular tear in the

atmosphere, measuring roughly two feet in diameter, and whilst its circumference remained

stable and uncompromising, the area within flickered like an old black and white television

that required tuning.

Lassa marvelled at her surroundings. She found herself standing in the middle of a large

heath in a spot dominated by low-growing shrubs with woody stems and narrow leaves, set

amongst the gentle rise and fall of hills and vales. Crisp, clean air rose up from the scrubby

vegetation and a dancing mist swirled about her. A little way off she could see sheep and

cattle grazing amid seemingly endless green fields divided by dry stone walls, and further still, an abundance of pretty purple heather grew alongside a crystal clear stream tumbling

over crags and fallen boulders. Overhead, swallows flitted in and out of the bushes, chasing

each other in knotting dives and loops. The view was so ruggedly beautiful, and so devoid of

human incursion, that it took Lassa's breath away.

All of a sudden a large hard-back book came flying through the portal, smacking Lassa

hard on the back of her head. She yelped, more from surprise than from pain, and crouched

down to pick up the offending item. She read the name of the title and its author out loud,

"Practical Chemistry by William A. Tilden." It was well read and dog-eared and its binding

was slack. The owner's inscription on the flyleaf read Philomena Dovetail.

Next to come flying through was a walnut box, housing a set of old scientific chemistry weights. Lassa ducked to avoid it and chuckled to herself before picking it up. Evidently the

Professor was becoming agitated.

"Professor, I'm okay!" she shouted, pitching her voice loudly enough so that it would carry

through the portal. She elevated the walnut box to waist level and hurled it back through. It

appeared to vanish in mid-flight. "Come and join me!"

Presently, a wrinkly brown hand poked tentatively through: Four bejewelled fingers and a

thumb twitching with nerves. Before Lassa could move or utter a sound, the hand was hastily

withdrawn.

Lassa gave a heavy sigh and placed her hands on her hips. She clicked her tongue

impatiently.

"Professor!" she bellowed. "You simply must come! You just won't believe your eyes!"

Philomena's hand re-appeared, more boldly this time, followed by a forearm, then the

rounding of a shoulder. Lassa saw her chance. Without any hesitation she seized a hold of

the arm and yanked hard and fast, pulling Philomena through the portal with all her might.

Philomena slid through the portal to land on her bottom on the ground with a wallop. She

sat up quickly in shock, dragging air into her lungs with colossal gulps. She glanced around

fearfully, her raven eyes as wide open as her mouth.

"Buckles and bootlaces! Where are we?" she asked. She was breathless and scared, but

otherwise quite unharmed.

"I think it's more a question of <u>when</u> are we," Lassa replied matter-of-factly.

Philomena rose unsteadily to her feet, her shoulders heaving as she gulped air in desperate mouthfuls.

"But that's impossible!" she countered. She pushed at the bottom of her spectacles which had slipped uncomfortably low on her nose. "Simply impossible," she repeated in a faraway voice, looking around her.

"After what I've seen today, nothing seems impossible anymore," Lassa said quietly.

Philomena surveyed her surroundings with disbelieving eyes. Her breathing was more regular now.

"Okay," she said calmly. "In that case, when are we?"

The sound of church bells filled the air, low and sweet like a call to prayer. Lassa turned.

In the distance, before the trees thickened into woods, she could see wreaths of smoke rising into the sky, marking a village or a town.

"I'm going to find out," she said regarding Philomena challengingly. She waited for her to

voice her condemnation of the idea, but, to her surprise, nothing was said. "Are you

coming?"

Beside her, Philomena nodded mutely.

Before setting off they marked out the entrance of the portal. They used branches and

twigs collected from the fringes of the heath to fashion a large cross on the ground.

"X marks the spot," Lassa said as she brushed her hands together and stepped back to

admire their handiwork. "Do you think it's good enough? We can't afford to lose sight of

our only path home."

Philomena swept a lock of unruly grey hair away from her forehead and out of her eyes.

"Yes, that should do the trick," she said with a satisfied nod of her head.

They tramped across the heath, through wetland plants, bramble and bilberry, then on

further to negotiate the muddy, potholed fields. A charm of goldfinches flew ahead of them,

twittering from tree to tree, and a vivid red fox centred across the field with a moorhen in its

mouth.

It wasn't long before they stumbled on lush green pastures, busy with grazing sheep on one

side and a herd of curious cows on the other. The cows stared at them with their big,

beautiful brown eyes, either mooing or chewing the cud as the Professor and Lassa passed by.

Soon they encountered a clear gravel path that ran between moss-covered walls and they followed it, not knowing what to expect at its terminus, their minds open to all possibilities.

A roe deer loped silently out of the wood. It paused for a moment on the path, regarded them

dispassionately, then trotted off into the woodland without any great sense of urgency.

Having lived on a neglected urban housing estate all her life, such rural delights left Lassa

with a sense of well-being and wonder.

Eventually they reached the end of the gravel path. It terminated at the border of a bustling

market town that was full of life and noise. The air was thick with the smell of smoke and

poverty. Carts and carriages rattled over the cobbles and a thousand pairs of feet pounded the

pavement. People in Old Worlde dress milled around, going about their day to day tasks. The

majority of them worse dark, scruffy clothes of sack cloth, buckram and wool, whilst a handful, the more affluent, were dressed impeccably in silks; the gentlemen wore breeches

and extravagant waistcoats with gilt metal buttons; the gentlewomen wore sack-back, open-

front petticoats made from damask worn over hooped underskirts.

Much of the activity was centred in the vicinity of the village quadrangle, a large cobbled

square surrounded by thatched roof buildings, where tens of people congregated there to hear

hawkers peddling their wares.

"Gather near, see my silver shoe-buckles, silver and dandy," one could be heard to cry.

"The finest canes, pinchbecks, sealing wax and quills. Come and see!" cried another.

Meanwhile, others were crowding around a man imprisoned in a large board with hinges;

his head, arms and legs held fast by a pillory. Children were running around him, laughing and pelting rotten eggs, stones and other missiles in his direction.

At the same time a second man was being taken down from a pillory to indignant

shouts and execrations from the crowd. He was begrimed with unpleasantly smelling

tomatoes and cabbage leaves. A more miserable wretch Lassa had never seen.

Lassa and Philomena continued to mingle with the villagers largely unnoticed, but both

were conscious of the fact that their 21st Century attire would soon attract unwanted attention.

Lassa's clothes, in particular, were beginning to draw curious glances and exchanges: Her

regulation school uniform of blazer and grey pleat skirt, together with her school rucksack,

heavily decorated with Pokemon iron-on patches, emoji pins and badges, were out of

place to say the very least.

"We need to find something more suitable to wear," Lassa said in a low voice.

Philomena nodded in agreement.

They quickly retreated behind an alehouse and dragged garments indiscriminately down

from the washing line that was stretched above the yard there.

In her haste Lassa displaced a small wooden crate beneath a window sill and as it scraped

across the stone floor, the rattle it made alerted a sleeping dog that was leashed to a post. It

was roused immediately, hackles raised, canines bared, and it sprang to its feet to pull at its

leash towards her. Lassa stood stock still in horror, but the yapping dog could not reach her

and it yelped as it was pulled back, the rope taut about its thick, muscled neck.

Philomena tugged at the sleeve of Lassa's blazer.

"Come on!" she urged her. "We've made enough noise to wake the dead!"

But Lassa was rooted to the spot with fear, staring at the enormous snarling dog standing

just inches away, its back arched, its bark becoming progressively louder and louder.

"Come on Lassa!" Philomena pressed her, more urgently now.

A door at the back of the inn groaned open and a thick-set woman with warts and facial

hair appeared, red-faced and angry.

"Geroffa my land!" she hollered from the doorstep, swinging a rolling pin. "Geroffa my

land, d'you hear?"

Lassa pulled herself together and without a backward glance she hotfooted it after the

Professor, who had already scarpered with a bundle of clothes tucked under her arms.

Together they ran across a field through a wood into a deserted barn in a clearing. Here they changed into their newly acquired garments, stuffing their own unceremoniously into

Lassa's school rucksack, which they then hid beneath a stack of hay in the corner.

They were almost fully dressed when they heard people approaching the barn at speed.

Philomena acted first, dragging Lassa up a ladder into the hayloft. They crept agonisingly

slowly over to the edge, careful not to rustle the hay that was spread thinly all around them,

and looked over. Philomena put a finger to her lips and Lassa shuffled involuntarily. Neither

of them said a word.

A young man and woman entered the barn, laughing and holding hands. They closed the

barndoor behind them and began to kiss each other passionately until the man eventually bent

down to scoop the woman up into his arms and carry her over to the stack of hay in the

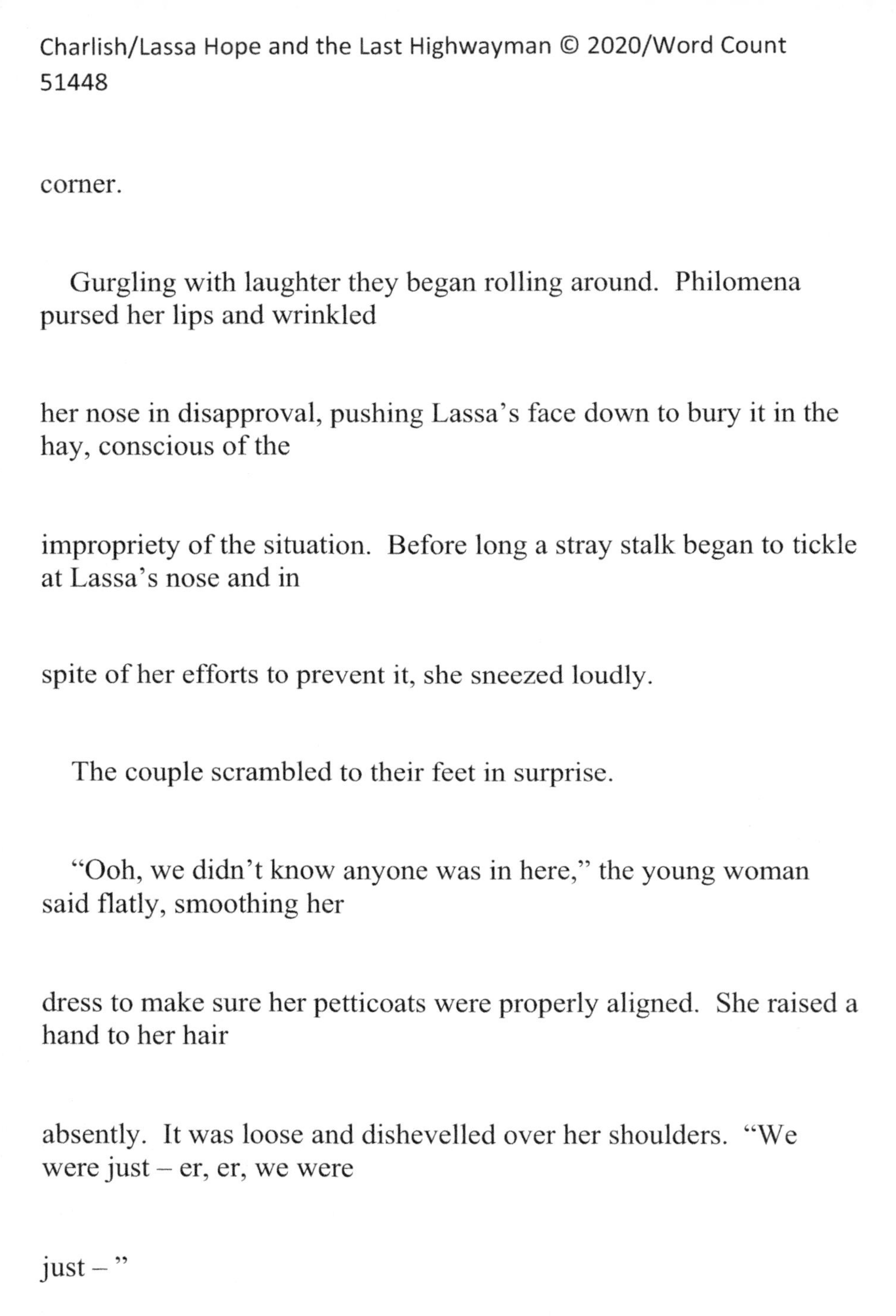

corner.

Gurgling with laughter they began rolling around. Philomena pursed her lips and wrinkled

her nose in disapproval, pushing Lassa's face down to bury it in the hay, conscious of the

impropriety of the situation. Before long a stray stalk began to tickle at Lassa's nose and in

spite of her efforts to prevent it, she sneezed loudly.

The couple scrambled to their feet in surprise.

"Ooh, we didn't know anyone was in here," the young woman said flatly, smoothing her

dress to make sure her petticoats were properly aligned. She raised a hand to her hair

absently. It was loose and dishevelled over her shoulders. "We were just – er, er, we were

just – "

The young man beside her shifted uncomfortably on his feet. Beads of sweat were forming

on his red and embarrassed face.

"We were just – " He hemmed and coughed. "We saw the barndoor open and thought we

ought to look in to check, to make sure everything was okay." He wrung his hands in

agitation. "We didn't mean no harm, honest we didn't."

Philomena and Lassa descended the ladder.

The woman refastened the eyelets of her bodice with quivering fingers.

"You won't – " - she started, her hazel eyes imploring Philomena - " - you won't tell my

father, will you?" She was small and blonde and exceedingly pretty, aged around sixteen

years old, with pearly-white even teeth and skin as smooth as velvet. "You won't will you?"

She held her breath. "Oh do promise you won't!" she said anxiously.

Philomena approached the man and woman kindly.

"My lips are sealed," she said with a conspiratorial wink.

"Thank you," the man said with feeling, looking relieved. He wiped the palm of his hand

down his breeches and extended it. "The name's Jacob," he said. "Jacob Campion."

Philomena accepted his outstretched hand and shook it.

"Philomena Dovetail," she said cheerfully in return. She gesticulated towards Lassa.

"And this is Lassa Hope, my – my – my twelve year old niece," she said, choosing her words

carefully.

Lassa flashed Philomena a sanctimonious glare.

"Actually, Aunt, I'm thirteen," she pointed out stiltedly.

"I'm Lydia," the young woman introduced herself. "Who are you two anyway?" she asked, eyeing Philomena and Lassa curiously as though seeing them for the first time. "And

what are you doing in Mr Groombridge's barn wearing nothing but your under garments?"

Philomena and Lassa looked at each other. Both were dressed in a fine white linen vest

and pantaloons. White lace caps sat awkwardly on their heads.

Lassa doubled up with laughter.

"You look like a bottle of milk!" she said to Philomena, chortling.

Philomena grinned.

"I suppose I do look a bit ridiculous," she said.

"Were you stopped by Dan Dandy?" Jacob asked suddenly in a voice louder than

necessary.

Philomena and Lassa exchanged bemused glances.

"The highwayman," Jacob illumined. "You must have heard of him. He's a dreadful villain, notorious in these parts. Perhaps you're not from round here?"

Lassa heaved a dramatic sigh.

"Alas, yes, we were held up by the rogue you speak of," she said gravely, thinking fast on her feet. "We were travelling along the road to Rugeley when we were ambushed. He stripped us of our upper garments and forced us to hand over our jewellery."

The professor cast Lassa a withering look. She makes Kate Winslet look like just another extra in a B-movie, she thought to herself wryly.

"The scoundrel!" cried Jacob and Lydia in unison, their eyes registering shock.

"He fired a musket and the shot startled our horses," Lassa continued. "They ran off with our coach in tow, leaving us half-dressed and stranded, miles from home."

Lassa gave a low moan for theatrical effect. She was glad she had seen repeats of Dick

Turpin, a 1980s TV show showcasing the swashbuckling adventures of the legendary

highwayman by the same name. She and Pops had often watched it on UK Gold and they

had both enjoyed the British drama series immensely.

Philomena rolled her eyes. Lassa could win an Oscar for this performance.

Lydia reached inside the bust of her bodice and pulled out a small, crumpled handkerchief.

She pressed a corner gently to Lassa's eyes, despite them clearly being dry.

"There, there," she said soothingly.

Jacob's lips thinned into an angry line.

"What an ordeal!" he exclaimed. "Dan Dandy needs a good horse-whipping!"

Lydia returned her handkerchief to her bodice and moved back.

"Well, you both need some clothes," she announced, blinking rapidly. "You can't walk

about like that, it's positively indecent." She turned to Jacob. "I'll fetch some at once."

Jacob indicated with a slight nod of his head that this was the right thing to do, so Lydia

turned on her heel and left them, the hem of her tan dress making a course scraping sound

across the floor of the barn as she moved.

Jacob sat himself heavily down on the floor and leant his back against a haystack. He

gestured for Philomena and Lassa to join him as he did so.

"My Lydia won't be long," he said with good cheer.

"You're both being very kind," Philomena said earnestly.

Jacob studied Philomena and Lassa through narrowed eyes. He was attractive in a boyish,

clean-cut way. Trim and muscular, with sandy coloured hair and big brown eyes, he had an

infectious smile that made him instantly extremely likeable and easy to warm to.

"So, you say you were travelling to Rugeley?" he prompted.

"Yes, we have family there," Lassa replied quickly and immediately felt embarrassed.

Lying did not come easily to her. "Tell us more about this fellow Dan Dandy that you speak

of," she said, changing the subject.

Jacob folded his arms. "Well," he began, puffing himself up a little, "Dan Dandy has been

terrorising the highways in this area for a good year or more – "

"A year or more?" Philomena interjected. "So that would mean – that would mean that he

has been terrorising the highways since – since – "

She paused, waiting hopefully for Jacob to fill in the gap.

Jacob did not disappoint. "Since 1764," he revealed.

A small gasp escaped Lassa's lips and her heart began to beat wildly in her ribcage. She

looked across at the professor. She was as white as her linen pantaloons, and her mouth was

agape.

"It's 1765?" Lassa said finally.

Jacob regarded Lassa as though she was the village idiot.

"Yes. It. Is," he said slowly for her benefit. "You must be suffering from shock," he said

at last, explaining away the young girl's odd behaviour. He sat bolt upright. "I'll fetch the

doctor!"

"No!" Philomena placed a hand on Jacob's shoulder to prevent him from upping and leaving. She gave a small reassuring smile. "We're fine, just a little shaken, that's all. There

really is no need to concern the doctor."

Jacob relaxed back against the stack.

"If you're sure," he said, his voice filled with uncertainty.

"We're sure," Lassa told him.

"Everything's fine," Philomena added.

"You were telling us about Dan Dandy," Lassa reminded him. "Is that his real name?"

Jacob shook his head and gave a small laugh.

"Nobody knows Dan Dandy's real name except Dan Dandy himself," he remarked affably.

"The locals gave him the name on account of his popularity with the gentlewomen he robs.

They seem to idolise him. He has a certain charm. His manners, it seems, are impeccable as far as the gentlewomen are concerned. He once insisted on kissing one of his lady victims on

the hand, after robbing her husband of his last guinea!" He shot Philomena and Lassa a

rueful glance, taking in their ill-fitting undergarments. "Evidently he lost his manners when

he held up your stagecoach!"

Lassa felt herself flush crimson over a myriad of freckles.

"Absolutely," she agreed, not looking him in the eye.

"I think he's a crook!" Jacob hissed. "Noble! Charming! Pah!" His voice boomed around

the barn. "He's nothing short of a common and lowly thief!" He looked down at his feet,

suddenly feeling more than a little foolish at his outburst. "I mean, what's noble about

somebody who robs others of their worldly possessions? What's charming about somebody who terrorises others, putting the fear of God into them? Eh? You tell me that."

Lassa's mind flashed momentarily back to thoughts of Clare Fox.

"Nothing at all," she lamented.

Jacob went on to recount tales of Dan Dandy's exploits for a further twenty minutes or

more. With an audience clearly captivated and hanging onto his every word, he embellished

and exaggerated every rumour that had ever circulated the village with an overwhelming

relish.

The description of Dan Dandy was vague to say the least. Aside from the fact that he rode

a white horse with distinctive black markings, and wore a tri-pointed hat, leather eye mask

and a black neckerchief to conceal his face from the eyes down, very little else was known

about him.

Lydia returned presently with an armful of dark coloured ladies' apparel. She had been

running hard and fast and was out of breath with the exertion. Her cheeks glowed brick-red

and were damp with perspiration.

"I was as quick as I could have been," she said apologetically, collapsing against a

haystack next to Lassa. "I've brought you a robe belonging to my sister. She's thirteen too."

She rolled out an empire line russet coloured dress for Lassa's appraisal.

"Oh it's lovely!" Lassa said in delight. "Thank you!"

Lydia looked pleased.

"And these are for you, Miss Dovetail – a coif, a petticoat, a skirt and a bodice. They all

belong to my mother. I fancy you and she are of similar proportions." She held up the skirt by the waistband. "They're old; she won't miss them."

Lassa and Philomena accepted the garments gratefully and went up into the hayloft to get

changed.

Jacob made a discreet exit.

"We need to find you lodgings" Lydia called up to them, her voice reverberating around

the rafters. "You will not be able to continue your journey to Rugeley today."

Philomena and Lassa stopped to stare at each other. They had no plans to stay in the 18th

Century overnight.

Philomena swallowed hard. "That won't be necessary, Lydia," she called out.

She began to descend the rickety ladder, but as her foot ventured out onto the top rung, the

old dead wood snapped under the weight of her body. Instinctively she reached out and grabbed a hold of the ledge of the hayloft, frantically trying to regain a foothold on the

buckled ladder.

Lassa screamed. "Professor!"

She hung her shoulders over the ledge and outstretched her arm. But it was too late. The

ladder broke away from the wall and Philomena lost her grip on the ledge.

Lassa could do nothing but watch helplessly as Philomena fell back, crashing down hard

on the uneven barn floor below.

Chapter Four

Introducing The Menzies

The doctor stood stiff backed and sombre.

"She is gravely ill," he said without preamble. He was a stout man, full bearded and

spectacled "Her condition is dire."

Lassa looked down at her feet, her face crumbling like a Danish pastry.

"Is she going to die?" Her voice was barely a whisper.

The doctor looked across at Philomena where she lay against pillows heaped high on the

bed. She was motionless and silent and her breathing was ragged.

"Only time will tell, I'm afraid," he imparted, his expression solemn. He replaced his

tricorn hat. "I'll call again tomorrow afternoon," he promised, and with a courteous farewell

nod, he left the room.

Following her fall from the hayloft earlier, Philomena had been carefully and quickly

transferred to Lydia's house by means of an old brewer's cart Jacob had borrowed from the innkeeper at The Staff and Shepherd. The mile long journey had been a bumpy one, largely

made across open, rutted ground, but Philomena had seemed unconcerned, lying unconscious

and unmoving in Lassa's arms for the duration.

Thick blood had matted her grey hair, dying the petals of the daisy entwined there a

crimson red. An ankle had turned at an awkward angle beneath her and looked swollen and

bruised, and her exposed lower arms were scratched and grazed.

She had been a most fearful sight, and Lassa had been thankful to eventually arrive at

Lydia's house, whereupon Jacob had immediately dashed off to fetch the doctor.

Lydia's other, Mary, was approaching Lassa now with a small, reassuring smile.

"I'm sure she will be absolutely fine," she said comfortingly, curling a gentle arm around

Lassa's shoulders. "Trust in the Lord."

She was a slightly built woman in her late forties, kind-looking and softly spoken. Her face was ashen and heavily lined and her hair was the colour of charcoal with just a smattering of grey.

She had welcomed Lassa and the injured Philomena into her home without reservation or query, hastening Lydia and Lydia's younger sister Esme to make up the bed in the spare room.

"I hope you're right," Lassa replied softly. Her hazel eyes did not deviate their gaze from Philomena's prostrate form. "May I stay with her a little while please?"

Mary nodded at Lassa and gestured to the chair at the bedside. Lassa slid into the chair and took a hold of Philomena's cold, wrinkled hand to warm it in her own. A single tear

rolled down her cheek. Mary smiled sadly and took her leave of the room, allowing Lassa to

maintain her vigil alone.

The room was darkened by heavy curtains and the bed upon which Philomena slept was

large and wooden with an elaborately curved headboard, a feather mattress and vast woollen

covers. The walls were covered in religious paintings, wooden crosses and tapestries.

Lassa knew that Philomena would be safe and well cared for here, and yet at the same time

she knew that the care she would receive at home, back in her own time, would be far

superior and more conducive to a speedier recovery. Since Philomena could not be moved

however, Lassa was also aware that her only option was to sit tight and wait until she was well again. In the meantime, she felt alone and scared, and utterly powerless.

*

The light was beginning to fade outside the pretty chocolate-box cottage, with its thatched

roof and whitewashed walls, trailing ivy and smoking chimney pots, and Lassa was growing

tired. It had been an exhausting day.

Lassa's thoughts turned to her grandparents, Ern and Nance. They would be expecting

her home from school shortly. Her grandmother would be checking on the meat and straining

the vegetables round about now; Pops would be sitting in his armchair watching the news on

the television, shaking his head and tutting at reports of further discord in the Middle East.

Both would be longing to greet her with a hug and a smile, keen to hear how her day had

passed.

They would be frantic with worry when Lassa did not return to kick off her shoes and hurl

her rucksack into the corner of the hall, as was her habit. Lassa's heart was heavy, If only

there was a way of reaching them, to let them know she was okay.

Philomena stirred momentarily in her sleep, mumbling incoherently. Lassa reached across

and mopped her fevered brow.

"Professor?" she prompted, her voice low. "Professor, it's me, Lassa Hope. Can you hear

me?"

There was no response. Even the incoherent mumblings had ceased.

Lassa sat back in her chair, her expression one of concern. Though the Professor's breathing was more regular now it was still shallow and her pulse was only tolerably strong. Her lips were dry and slightly parted, and her hair was pushed back from her forehead. She showed no signs of regaining consciousness, and Lassa wondered if she ever would. She let out an involuntary, quiet choked sound and dropped her head in her hands.

The Professor couldn't die, she thought to herself. She simply couldn't. It would be too great a loss to the school – to the world – and to her. She was such an intelligent, caring woman who still had much to offer. After all, she had created a portal into the past, albeit inadvertently. Where others had failed before her, Professor Philomena Dovetail had succeeded. She would be awarded a Nobel Prize for sure.

Having read H G Wells' science fiction novella The Time Machine a year or so ago, Lassa

had considered the possibilities of time travel, but not until now had she imagined that it

would one day prove to be a reality, that somehow different space times really could co-exist

and could be visited by means of a wormhole. Although H G Wells had dreamt up a time

travelling contraption, where an intrepid operator would pull a lever, turn a dial and

materialize in a time when dinosaurs roamed the earth, Philomena appeared to have created

the wormhole itself, a portal into another dimension and time. The chemical reaction she

had stumbled upon had quite literally opened up a new world of opportunity, and Lassa was

overwhelmed at the thought that she was now living in it.

Lassa heard footsteps ascending the narrow stairs outside the room and rose from the chair.

Lydia entered moments later. She looked anxious.

"How is she?" she asked. She walked over to Lassa and stood at her shoulder, her mouth a

grim line.

"There's been no change." Lassa shrugged off the frightened feeling inside with a

nervous laugh. "But I'm sure she'll wake up soon, demanding something hot to eat and

grouching over her sore head."

Lydia gave a light laugh. "Yes, I'm sure of that too."

The room fell quiet for a moment.

"Mother has prepared a meal," Lydia said at last. "We would like you to come and join

us."

"No, thank you, I'm – "

"We insist," Lydia said firmly. "You must eat!"

Lassa blinked twice, then shook her head. "No, I really should stay with my aunt."

"We won't take no for an answer," Lydia said. She crossed her arms over her chest and

looked at Lassa mutinously through long thick lashes. "You'll be no good to your aunt if you

become ill yourself."

Lassa nodded resignedly. She knew the Professor would not miss her, and it would be

hours before she woke. Besides which, sudden thoughts of a roast chicken dinner,

compounded by a rumbling tummy, told her it was time to eat. She and Lydia descended the

staircase and entered into a small dining room, illuminated by beeswax candles and a fire that

raged in the hearth. The ceiling was low with massive oak beams and the stone-flagged floor was well swept and highly polished, gleaming iridescently in the light of the flickering

flames.

In the centre of the room, seven high backed chairs were positioned around a long wooden

table. The charger, at the head of the table, was unoccupied, although a plate and a pewter

goblet had been set there.

Esme was seated at the table, along with her sisters, eight year old twins Temperance and

Elizabeth, two elfin faced girls with golden tresses that lapped about their shoulders. All

three were eating greedily from bowls, spooning what appeared to be an oatmeal and butter

mix greedily into their evidently hungry little mouths.

Lassa took her seat next to Esme, and Mary came forward to serve her food. The heat in

the tiny dining room had caused a bead of sweat to break out on her forehead and her normally sallow complexion was heightened to the red colour of a turkey's wattle. Strands of

dark hair had escaped from the knot to which she had that morning confined it, and her

small, slim figure was enveloped in a large apron, which was stained and creased.

"It's not the finest of food you'll ever eat," she said, wiping her hands on her apron, "but it

is hot and it is plentiful."

Lassa looked at Lydia, who was already ravenously tucking into her bowl of gruel; then at

Esme and the twins, who were just about finishing theirs off, their bowl raised high to their

mouths as they licked noisily at the bottom.

The gruel looked and smelt awful, but Lassa was famished, having not eaten since

breakfast, and so she wolfed it down gratefully. Her bowl was empty in seconds.

Mary served the girls a second helping, Lassa included, then took her own seat at the table.

"Lydia tells me you were held up by Dan Dandy on your way to Rugeley" she said

between mouthfuls of food. "Do you have family there?"

By her very nature, Lassa hated lying. These were good people and they did not deserve

untruths. But by the same token she knew she could not tell them the facts. They would

neither believe her, nor comprehend.

"My uncle lives there."

"Mrs Dovetail's husband?"

"He's – I – yes, he's her husband." Lassa was a bad liar. "You have a lovely home," she

quickly changed the subject.

Mary washed down her meal with a beaker of water and shrugged her shoulders dismissively.

"It's a roof over our heads," she said dolefully, giving Lassa the impression that she was

not entirely satisfied with her lot in life.

Suddenly the heavy wooden door of the dining room swung open and Lassa turned to see a

man standing on the threshold. He was tall and muscular and his hair was long and dark,

drawn back behind his head by a black ribbon. He wore a leather apron and a leather tool

belt, and from his fatigued expression it was apparent to Lassa that he had just finished

a hard day's work.

Immediately upon seeing his daughters, his lips curled into a happy smile.

"Father!" the twins cried delightedly in unison, darting across the room towards him.

The man reached down to scoop them up into his strong arms.

"Ah, Temperance and Elizabeth, my sweet girls," he greeted them tenderly. "Have you

been good for your mother?"

The twins giggled mischievously. "Of course we have, father!" Temperance told him.

"We're always good for mother, father," added Elizabeth with mock indignation.

The man chortled and his whole body shook. He lowered his daughters to the ground and

walked across to his wife.

"Is this true, Mary?" he asked with a wink, attempting to draw her into his arms.

"Yes it is and no – no, you don't!" she protested good naturedly, backing away from him.

"Your hands are filthy and you smell of burnt hoof!" She allowed him to kiss her chastely on

the cheek. "Now, wash up for dinner, my love, we have a visitor."

He dutifully exited the room,, chortling still.

Touched by the obvious devotion to his family, Lassa warmed to him at once.

"That's my father," Lydia told Lassa, unable to contain the pride in her voice. "He's a

blacksmith. He works at the forge in the village."

The blacksmith returned presently, looking tired and drawn, and plonked himself down in

the charger. He gave a long sigh and stretched his legs out in front of him, rubbing at his

temples.

"Are you unwell, my love?" Mary asked him with concern.

"Just weary," he reassured her. "I must have nailed on a hundred shoes today."

Mary served him his meal and poured him some water. "You work too hard," she said.

"Don't fuss, woman," he said genially. He turned to Lassa. "Do you think anyone will

ever tell me your name, young lady?" he said with a wink. "Or will I have to guess?"

Lassa laughed.

"I'm Lassa Hope," she told him a little shyly. "My aunt had an accident in Mr

Groombridge's barn. Lydia very kindly brought her here so that a doctor could attend to

her."

The man smiled at Lydia, and the light from the fire lashed off his teeth.

"Ah, my kind, beautiful Lydia," he said.

Acknowledging the compliment, Lydia moved behind her father and kissed the top of his

head.

"I trust your aunt is well?" the man continued through narrowed eyes.

"She's resting upstairs, father," Lydia interjected. "Dr Calder says she shouldn't be

moved."

The man smiled. "Ah, if she's in John Calder's hands, then she's in good hands. Your

aunt will be fine," he remarked. He stretched his arms high above his head and yawned.

"Mary, my love, I think I'll retire for the night."

"So soon?" Mary queried. "But you've barely touched your supper."

"It's been an exhausting day," he replied. "All I want to do is to sleep."

He kissed his wife on the forehead and made for the door.

"Goodnight, father!" cried Esme, Temperance and Elizabeth simultaneously.

The man turned. "Goodnight, girls," he said affectionately. He raised a hand in a last farewell, then left the room.

Mary sighed sadly and began to clear the table. "Moses works too hard," she muttered,

chiefly to herself.

"Moses?" Lassa prompted.

"My husband, Moses Menzies," Mary replied, sighing still. "He works such long hours. I

rarely see him these days. He's either working or sleeping."

Lassa shivered involuntarily, the sound of the name sending a chill and a strange searing

heat through her body concurrently. <u>Moses Menzies</u>. Lassa felt the colour draining away

from her face, paling it to a deathly hue.

<u>Moses Menzies. The last man to be hanged at Gibbet Hill.</u>

Lassa cast her eyes upwards, along the stairs, to watch Moses climbing them, slowly but surely, before disappearing into the floor above. She grew paler, if that were possible. She was lodging with a highwayman!

Her heart hammered in her chest and her hands shook. Questions ran through her mind in quick succession. Could Moses Menzies be Dan Dandy, the infamous highwayman? Or had he been hanged an innocent man? After all, records showed that he had sworn his innocence right until the very end. Could it be that Moses had been telling the truth?

This was all beginning to get too much for Lassa. The pounding in her heart grew louder and louder, so loud she feared that Mary and the girls would hear it, She jumped to her feet, her head spinning with the effort, and scraped her chair backwards.

"May I – may I be – may I be excused from the table please? I - " Her voice started to break. "I want to check on my aunt."

"Yes of course," Mary said with a look of motherly concern.

Without delay, Lassa ran from the room and up the stairs into the room where Philomena

was sleeping.

The Professor's complexion had altered. She was even pastier than when Lassa had last

seen her. Her eyes opened briefly when Lassa took a seat at her side, but they did not register

recognition, nor surprise at their surroundings. Lassa took her hand in hers. It was limp and

clammy. <u>Oh, if only she would wake up and talk to her!</u>

"Wake up, Professor, please!" Lassa beseeched her. "I'm afraid we're in an awful mess!"

But Philomena remained still and unhearing.

Chapter Five

A Stagecoach Robbery

Lassa chose not to sleep in the bed Mary had made up for her in Esme's room. Instead she

slept in the chair at Philomena's bedside. It was hard and uncomfortable and Lassa tossed

and turned all night. By morning, her body ached from top to toe, and a cutting draught the

curtains at the window were too short to stop had left her with a painful crick in her neck.

She walked over to the window and drew back the curtains, watching the early morning

sun rise. The reds and ambers hit her eyes and made her blink sharply, but she did not look

away.

A threatening thunderstorm drew a little closer in a far-off rumble of sound. The rain

would come soon.

"Rainbow weather," Lassa mused as the sunshine began to filter in.

There had been no change in Philomena's condition during the night. She still lay without

movement on the bed. Her breathing faltered raggedly and her colour was grey.

Lassa made a silent prayer for the Professor to make a speedy recovery. She wanted

nothing more than to see her well again – and to go home, back to her grandparents, Ern and

Nance. She missed them so much it pained her to think of them and the worrying she was

causing.

There was a knock at the door, a cautious knock, followed by a call of Lassa's name. It

was Mary's voice.

"Come in," Lassa said, moving away from the window.

Mary entered, wearing an unflattering white apron over a plain black dress that allowed only the tips of her shoes to be seen. A white cap sat on her head. She looked anxious.

"Has there been any change?" she asked, glancing over at Philomena.

"None," replied Lassa with a plaintive tremor. A tear trickled down her cheek and she

wiped it away with the back of her hand.

Mary approached Lassa to envelop her in the circle of her arms. She squeezed her gently.

"She will get better," she promised, but the tone of her voice betrayed her uncertainty.

Lassa welcomed the embrace, and for just a few moments she just stood there, allowing

herself to be comforted. "Thank you," she said.

"For what?" Mary asked at Lassa's shoulder, raising a thin and inquisitive brow.

Lassa moved out of Mary's arms and took a step backwards. Her tears had now subsided,

leaving clear salty streams down her face that ended at her chin.

"For your kindness," she said simply.

Mary laughed lightly and her dark eyes twinkled.

"We Menzies have a golden rule, Lassa," she told her. "Do unto others as you would have them do unto you."

With a sudden hiss, the rain came; fat globules of water that bounced and splattered off the window pane. Nonetheless the sun continued to break through the clouds and the most beautiful rainbow appeared, a tremulous arc of the most resplendent colours, shimmering in the sky, a sparkling brook at its beginning and a copse of ash trees at its end.

"How lovely!" Mary exclaimed. She clapped her hands and smiled delightedly.

Lassa felt suddenly happier.

"It's a sign," she said breathlessly. "A sign that my aunt will soon be on her feet again."

They turned in unison to look at the Professor. Her eyes were now half open, and for a

moment it appeared that she was indeed beginning to emerge from her deep sleep. But she

did not.

"You could be right, Lassa," Mary said. "We shall know more when the doctor has seen

her. I am expecting him to call after church this morning."

Lassa felt hopeful for the first time since the accident.

*

Before long Lassa and Mary went downstairs. Lassa had washed and dressed, and she felt

more optimistic and confident that the Professor would soon pull through.

In the sitting room they found Moses, poking wildly at the fire glowing gently in the grate.

He was respectfully dressed in his Sunday best; a navy frock coat, breeches, black stockings

and shoes with a small heel and silver buckles.

"Well, don't you look fine and dandy!" Mary teased him, smoothing down his coat tails.

Dandy. That one word haunted Lassa's thoughts and made her quake in fear. And yet –

somehow – she could not quite picture Mr Menzies leading a double life: One as the

immaculately attired, hard-working father that stood before her now; the other as the

dastardly highwayman that had terrorised the roads for an entire year. It just didn't add up

somehow.

"I won't tolerate a casual approach to worship, Mary," he said, a little piously. "We must

all be ordered and reverent in the house of the Lord."

The flames of the fire flew up a little higher.

"Christ died to save all souls, Moses, whether you be well dressed or not, rich or poor,"

Mary reminded him. She took a turn poking at the fire, making the flames leap right up the

chimney. "I'm sure he would think no different of you if you dressed in rags! Before the

Lord, we are all one and the same."

"So you won't be changing then?" Moses chided, knowing, as Lassa did, that she had

every intention of doing so.

Mary looked appalled. "Of course I'll be changing!" she huffed. "I can't go to church

looking like this! What would people think of me?

And without further ado, she haughtily left the room.

Moses chuckled. "Mary, Mary quite contrary," he quipped in a sing song voice.

Further doubts crept into Lassa's mind. Could the face of this obviously deeply religious man, who talked so earnestly of order and reverence, really be behind the mask of Dan Dandy? Certainly she was still highly suspicious of him. There's no smoke without fire, her grandmother Nance was often known to say.

"You will attend church with us, Lassa," Moses said kindly, but firmly, breaking the silence that had begun to linger.

Lassa risked a nod.

Moses sat down in a chair facing the fire. "Has your aunt's condition much improved?" he asked hopefully, sensitive to the tension in the atmosphere.

Lassa took a deep breath. She met Moses' eyes briefly, then lowered her gaze to the floor.

"She has not woken, sir," she said. Alone with this man she felt nervous, fretful even, despite his personable disposition and the fact that he had shown her nothing but kindness

and courtesy. But then hadn't Dan Dandy been so-named because of his courteous, gallant

and chivalrous behaviour towards the ladies? Lassa felt confused. None of it

made any sense.

Suddenly, dressed exquisitely in green, Lydia sauntered into the room, accompanied by her

sisters, Esme and the twins, who were equally as impeccably dressed. Moses complimented

them all on their appearance, and all four flushed instantly, flashing their father huge, proud

smiles.

Mary joined them presently, wearing a long grey-green dress comprising of two lengths of

fabric pinch-pleated at the waist. She had pulled back her long dark hair into a tight regimental bun, and a simple gold cross chain hung from her neck. She was much improved,

and when Moses saw her, he smiled his approval.

"Mary, you're a treat for the eyes!" he declared, clapping his hands. He snaked an arm

around her waist and pulled her close to kiss her on the cheek. "As beautiful now as the day

we were married."

Mary wriggled free, chuckling.

"Moses Menzies, you are incorrigible!" she said with mock reproach. "Now let's make a

move or we'll be late for the start of the service."

*

Scarcely a glimpse of the church could be seen until you were well within its gates, so thickly

was it embosomed in trees, but Lassa recognised it straight away. It was St Mary

Magdalene's and it still stood in Bott Lane in her own time, a rundown listed building that

had not been used since the Second World War, when it had suffered major bomb damage.

Here, in 1765, it had only been built some ten years previously, and it still looked brand new.

It was a small, handsome-looking church built from stone brick. It had a tower, which

housed a large bell, and a grand arched doorway with a solid looking wooden door. On her

approach, Lassa found herself admiring the beautiful stained glass windows, depicting both

the birth and the crucifixion of Christ, and realised with melancholy that these no

longer existed back in the 21st Century. She remembered that the few that had survived the air raids had been removed for security and safety reasons in 1997, and were now on a public

display in her local library. Indeed, as primary school pupil, Lassa had been on a trip to view

them there.

When they reached the porch of the church, a small group of people bade them good

morning. One face was familiar to Lassa. It was Jacob Campion. He was standing with an

older lady and gentleman, who Lassa assumed to be his parents, and was smartly dressed in

his best bib and tucker. His sandy coloured hair had been washed and trimmed, and was

neatly tied back behind his head with a black ribbon. Lassa thought he looked positively

dreamy.

For a short time the Menzies and the Campions discussed the poor weather and lamented upon the recent death of a mutual friend, before being hastened inside by the verger.

The Menzies took their seats on pews at the front of the church, to the right of the pulpit.

The Campions moved to the left. A coy, flirtatious exchange between Jacob and Lydia did

not go unmissed by Moses, who duly clipped his eldest daughter round the ear, scowling and

muttering something inaudible under his breath. Clearly he was not impressed. Lydia nursed

her sore ear and sulkily joined her family in lighting a candle to accompany their silent

prayers.

Lassa felt apprehensive. Having not attended church since she was three years old, when

she was a flower girl at her cousin's wedding, she was afraid of breaching worship etiquette.

Erring on the side of caution she mirrored everything that Lydia did and hoped that her

nerves did not give her away.

The service was held by Rector Samuel Tulliver, who spoke of the virtues of Godliness

and the path to righteousness, quoting the Gospels and the Psalms, which he plainly knew by

heart.

Lassa found it excruciatingly boring and would have nodded off, had it not been for Jacob

Campion's father, who snored so loudly throughout the entire sermon that she thought her

ears would bleed. Jacob's mother could be seen nudging him occasionally and he would

rouse briefly, snorting and snuffling, before promptly dozing off again. The children in

the congregation all found it highly amusing; the adults found it less so. They all shook their heads, clicked their tongues and puckered their brows in staunch disapproval.

Immediately after the service everyone bustled out of the church to congregate outside.

They were chittering and chattering animatedly with each other, laughing gaily. No-one

seemed in a particular hurry to get home.

All except Lassa. She was itching to get back to the Professor. She didn't quite know

what had possessed her to leave her in the first place. Admittedly Dr Calder's housemaid, a

pale slip of a girl with a gaunt bony face and hollow cheeks named Nelly, agreed to sit with

her, alleviating a little of Lassa's guilt. But what if the Professor woke up to find that Lassa

wasn't there at her side? The poor woman wouldn't have the first clue where she was. Lassa

mentally chastised herself for being so thoughtless.

"Well look who it is!" Moses sniffed.

Lassa's eyes traced his line of vision. He was glaring at a tall, prosperous looking

gentleman who stood conversing with the rector beneath a large elm. He was wearing a

tightly fitting patterned silk coat that was cut away to form curving tails, and breeches that

fastened below the knee. An attractive woman stood at his side, her arm hooked in his.

She too was as tastefully attired in silk, and an immense plumed hat topped her head.

"Who is he?" Lassa asked.

Moses glowered. "Mr Joseph Cruickshank," he said curtly and without

fondness. "He's a landowner who lives up at Urton Hall." He caught the eye of the

gentleman in question, but he did not look away. "And he owes me money."

Sensing the tension in the air, Mary steered her husband around so that he was facing her.

"Moses, we're still on church land," she remained him crossly, adding pertinently, "there's a

time and a place to talk about money, and it's not here and it's not now!"

"But he owes me three shillings!" Moses boomed. "I don't shoe horses for the love of it!

Back-breaking work it is too!" He regarded Joseph Cruickshank through narrowed, incensed

eyes. "Look at him in his fancy clothes! How dare he owe me money while I struggle to put

food on the table!"

Mary hushed her husband and placed a finger on his lips. "Not here, Moses!" she

admonished him, and she flashed a look that silenced him at once.

Lassa heard Joseph Cruickshank and his wife thank the rector for a wonderful service and bid him farewell before leaving, by means of a carriage, through the church gates and up the

dirt track towards the village.

Moses visibly relaxed after their departure and spoke freely with the other parishioners.

Both he and Mary appeared to be a very popular couple, as did their children, and Lassa felt

proud to be in their company.

The walk back to the Menzies cottage was wretched. The rain lashed down and the wind

blew strong, triggering the trees to wail an inhuman lamentation in the subdued brightness.

The mid-morning sky had turned to darkness, the light only fleetingly reappearing with brief

electric flashes that zigzagged across the heavens. Thunder crackled and boomed, causing

Lassa to jump involuntarily and to grab a hold of Lydia's hand. Together they gathered pace, their boots squelching through the newly created mud, whilst gunshot rain continued to

pepper the dirt track all about them.

By the time they reached home, Lassa, Moses, Mary, Lydia, Esme and the twins were all

completely wet through. Their hair was plastered to their scalps and the sides of their faces,

and droplets of rain water rolled off their noses and onto their chests. For a while they all

stood together in a circle, laughing uproariously at the sorry sights before them.

Lassa could not remember the last time she had laughed so hard.

Having first towelled herself dry by the crackling log fire in the sitting room, Lassa went

upstairs to call in on the Professor.

She found Dr Calder's housemaid Nelly sitting beside her bed, reading out loud to her

from a small leather-bound book. To Lassa's dismay, the Professor had still not regained consciousness.

Lassa thanked Nelly for her time and politely dismissed her from the room. She hoped that

Dr Calder would come soon, as she had promised; she was keen to hear what he thought of

the Professor's condition now, some twenty four hours after his last visit.

Then, just as Lassa had sat down in the chair that Nelly had vacated moments earlier,

Philomena stirred, moaning ever so slightly. Lassa's head shot up and she shuffled her chair

closer to the bed to take her hand. It lay limp in her own, and was a as light as a feather,

stippled with liver spots and with a lace-work of pulsating blue veins.

"Lassa?" Philomena's voice was scarcely a whisper, emitted from a throat that was so dry

the words cracked and broke. "Wh -where am I?"

The most timid flicker of hope awakened in Lassa's heart.

"Professor?" she whispered, her pulse quickening. "Professor, how are you feeling?"

After what felt like an eternity, Philomena finally spoke. "My mouth's dry."

Lassa fetched a beaker of water and tipped it gently to Philomena's parched lips.

"You had me worried, Professor," she said.

Philomena accepted the water gratefully.

"Where are we?" she asked again between small sips.

"At Lydia's home," Lassa replied. "When you fell from the hayloft, she and Jacob brought

you here in the back of an old brewer's cart."

Philomena groaned and raised a hand to her aching head.

"Buckles and bootlaces!" she gasped. "I thought it had all been a dream!"

There was a knock at the door and Mary entered, accompanied by Lydia, who was carrying

a steel pitcher of wild yellow flowers.

"She's awake!" Lydia cried out, almost dropping the pitcher in her surprise.

"How are you, Mrs Dovetail?" Mary asked. "You had a very nasty fall and gave your

niece quite a fright."

Philomena attempted to sit up, but she found she could not do so without Lassa's

assistance. Her head throbbed and her entire body was riddled with pain. Lassa plumped up

her pillow high against the headboard, and Philomena settled back onto it with a wince.

"I feel perfectly fine," Philomena said, but her strained, pale face told an altogether

different story.

"These are for you, Mrs Dovetail," Lydia told her, placing the pitcher of flowers down on

the dresser.

Philomena managed a small smile. "Thank you, my dear," she said. They're quite

lovely."

"We're expecting Dr Calder any moment," Mary told her. "He'll have you up on your feet

again in no time."

"Are you hungry, Mrs Dovetail?" Lydia asked.

"A little," Philomena replied.

Mary looked across at Lydia. "Come, let's fetch Mrs Dovetail a warm bowl of parsnip

soup and some bread." She smothered the covers around Philomena's body, telling her, "It

will do you the world of good."

Before leaving the room, Lydia took a long-stemmed flower from the pitcher and pushed it

gently into Philomena's hair.

"There, it suits you," she said.

Philomena was touched. "Thank you," she said earnestly.

"You're very welcome," Lydia told her as she and her mother quietly left the room.

"That was a sweet thing to do," Philomena said. "She must have noticed the daisy in my

hair yesterday."

Now that Philomena was sitting up, some of the colour had returned to her cheeks and

Lassa decided it was time to broach the subject of returning home.

"We must get you up on your feet again soon, Professor; we really do need to get home.

My grandparents must be worried sick," she said. "But it's not only that. I have reason to

believe that Lydia's father is a highwayman. And not just any highwayman. I believe him to

be none other than Dan Dandy." She lowered her voice surreptitiously. "Does the name

Moses Menzies mean anything to you?"

In spite of her pain, Philomena was intrigued.

"It rings a bell," she said.

"He was the last man to be hanged at Gibbet Hill, the site upon which our school now

stands."

"So?" Philomena prompted.

"He's Lydia's father," Lassa revealed. "He's a blacksmith by trade, but he leads a double

life – as a highwayman."

Philomena did not look convinced. "But you don't know that for sure? I mean, I

remember reading that he proclaimed his innocence right until the end."

"Well, no, I don't know that for sure," Lassa admittedly a little awkwardly. "But surely

they wouldn't have hanged him had he not been guilty?"

"No necessarily," Philomena said. "The judicial system hasn't always been as good as it is

in our day. There was no forensic science, DNA technology and fingerprinting techniques

for example. Many an innocent man or woman was hanged in the past."

"True," Lassa agreed unenthusiastically. She didn't want to believe that Moses was the

notorious highwayman who went by the name of Dan Dandy, but it was preferable to

believing that he had been gibbeted as an innocent man.

"Anyway, it wasn't just highwaymen that they hanged. Perhaps he was found guilty of

some other crime." Philomena shifted her body and she flinched in pain. "And besides, I

don't think I'll be going anywhere for a while," she said sadly, trying to find a position in

which she felt comfortable. "You must go home without me. I will follow on when I am

well enough."

"No!" The very thought was abhorrent to Lassa. "I won't leave you," she said with

resolve.

"If what you say is true, you could be in danger," Philomena reasoned. "Supposing Moses

Menzies realises that you know of his alter ego. He might – "

Lassa's thoughts revolved in a three hundred and sixty degree turnabout.

"But it might <u>not</u> be him" she protested. "After all, like you said, he pleaded his

innocence right until the very end, even as he was being walked to the gallows. He could

very well have been telling the truth!"

Philomena chortled heartily, causing her whole body to shake, then immediately regretted

it as a wave of pain washed over her. When she spoke it was not without effort. "Well, you

soon changed your tune," she declared.

"But I don't want to leave you," Lassa conveyed emotively, adding quietly, "I won't go."

Philomena sighed. She felt too weak to argue.

*

Dr Calder was late in calling in at The Menzies' house. He had been expected to arrive at just after two o'clock, but by four there was still no sign of him. Philomena had fallen back to sleep after having eaten her parsnip soup. She had only managed a few spoonfuls before she had begun to feel drowsy, and so Lassa had finished it off for her. It wasn't Heinz by any stretch of the imagination, but Lassa had felt ravenous and had lapped it up in five seconds flat.

At last Lassa heard a knock on the door of the cottage. She looked out of the window and, sure enough, she saw Dr Calder's carriage outside. Its two horses were neighing and whinnying in the bitter wind and unrelenting rain, and Lassa's heart went out to them as the sky discharged another deafening rumble.

Lassa brushed Philomena's cheek with her knuckles and dropped a soft kiss on her warm

skin, then left the room to join Mary and the rest of the family downstairs.

As she descended the staircase she heard loud voices talking excitedly from the sitting

room, and she stopped on the penultimate step, listening.

"It's an outrage, John!" She heard Moses bellow. "An absolute outrage!"

Lassa heard a collective mumbling of agreement.

"You're not wrong, Moses, my dear friend." It was Dr Calder and he sounded livid.

"Henry and Clarissa were frightened out of their wits! Thank the Lord the children were not

travelling with them on this occasion." His voice was punctuated by a shudder. "The sooner

this villain is apprehended the better!"

"It's happening all too frequently!" This time it was Lydia who spoke, her voice indignant

and shrill.

Lassa took a small, measured breath and tentatively entered into the room.

"Hello Lassa," Moses greeted her genially. He was sitting in the chair nearest to the fire,

smoking a half penny clay pipe. Mary and Lydia stood at his side, their expressions serious.

"Is anything wrong?" Lassa ventured bravely.

Moses rubbed his bristly chin. "Nothing that concerns you, Lassa," he said eithout

preamble.

Dr Calder snorted. "On the contrary Moses, it concerns everyone!"

Mary glanced apprehensively between her husband and the doctor.

"There's been another hold up," she revealed briskly. "Dr Calder's sister Clarissa and her

husband Henry Fairweather. They were travelling from Cheadle, when they were stopped on

the road leading into the village."

"They are spending the week with me," Dr Calder continued. "My sister needs to

convalesce following an illness."

"When did this happen?" Lassa asked.

"About an hour ago," Moses divulged begrudgingly. He had no wish to involve the

children for fear of scaring them. But Lassa seemed different somehow, more mature than

Esme, who was of a similar age, and certainly more worldy-wise.

All at once Lassa's heart was filled with a gladness at the sudden realisation of the truth.

Moses could not possibly be Dan Dandy! He had not left the cottage since returning from

church, not for one moment. But then why was he hanged? It just didn't make any sense.

"That's why I was so late getting here," Dr Calder said apologetically. "It took an age for

myself and Henry to calm poor Clarissa. She was distraught beyond words! I had heard that

Dan Dandy was a gallant scoundrel, mindful to a lady's delicate sensibilities, but my sister

refutes that most vehemently."

"What did he take from them, John?" Moses asked, briefly removing the clay pipe from

his mouth.

"A cameo brooch, dress rings and a diamond necklace that was a family heirloom. He

even tore the gilt buckles from Henry's coat!"

"He'll get his comeuppance," Lydia Said sagely.

"Not soon enough for my liking!" Dr Calder declared haughtily.

"I agree, John," Moses said, taking up his clay pipe again.

Esme and the twins entered the room then, serving to break up the conversation with their

fun and youthful exuberance. Mary motioned them out into the kitchen at once and Lydia

followed.

"Well, I'll talk no more of this today," said Dr Calder. "It's time I checked on

Mrs Dovetail, herself a victim of this darned villain!"

He made for the door.

"She has awoken, doctor," Lassa informed him.

"That is indeed excellent news," he said with good humour, in spite of his awful day.

“She’s made the first step towards a full recovery,” he added. And then he was gone.

Moses sucked at his pipe. “You’re very welcome to stay until your aunt is on her feet,

Lassa, no fear of that,” he told her with feeling.

“Th - thank you,” Lassa said, suddenly flustered. The Menzies were good people indeed.

She felt wracked with shame, thoroughly despising herself or ever thinking that Moses could

possibly be Dan Dandy, the infamous highwayman. “I don’t know how I will ever be able to

repay your kindness.”

“I wouldn’t hear of it!” declared Moses as though the thought appalled him.

“You’re all so very, very kind,” Lassa said sincerely.

“Supper’s ready!” Mary suddenly called for them. They followed the sound of her voice

into the dining room, where they found her ladling soup from a large pot.

Moses discarded his clay pipe and took his seat in the charger, licking his lips and smelling

his bowl. "Lassa, would you like to say Grace?" he said.

"Say Grace? Oh no! Thank you – no," she countered quickly, suddenly disconcerted.

"Oh, but you must, Lassa!" Lydia entreated her.

Esme, Temperance and Elizabeth starred at her expectantly, their eyes as wide as saucers.

Mary nodded to her and gave her an encouraging smile. Lassa swallowed hard. She had

never said Grace in her life. Indeed she had only ever heard Grace being said by Joe Ingles in

television re-runs of The Little House on the Prairie, which was one of her grandmother's

favourite programmes from the 1970s and which she herself had only ever watched half-

heartedly. How she wished she had paid more attention! For now she did not have the first notion of what to say or how to say it.

She put her hands together in prayer and closed her eyes. This part she knew. The

Menzies family followed her lead. Then she cleared her throat nervously, and with a sinking

feeling of doom, she slowly and sombrely proceeded to recite the lyrics to Angels by Robbie

Williams.

"When I'm feeling weak, and my pain walks down a one way street

I look above, and I know I'll always be blessed with love.

And as the feeling grows

She breathes flesh to my bones

And when love is dead

I'm loving angels instead.

And through it all she offers me protection, a lot of love and affection

Whether I'm right or wrong.

And down the waterfall, wherever it may take me

I know that life won't break me

When I come to call

She won't forsake me

I'm loving angels instead."

When Lassa opened her eyes, the Menzies were staring, no gawping at her, wholly

dumbfounded. It was Mary who spoke first.

"That was – um – er – very lovely, Lassa," she said.

"Very unique," Lydia said.

Moses did a lot of hemming and hawing, forever the traditionalist, but said nothing as he reached for the bread.

"Well I <u>liked</u> it," said Temperance coyly, smiling.

Lassa could feel the colour jetting to her neck and to her face.

"Thank you," she said. She hoped they wouldn't ask her to say Grace again; the only other

lyrics she knew were those to <u>Poker Face</u> by Lady Gaga.

Just as Lassa had finished eating her supper – more parsnip soup – Dr Calder reappeared,

having looked in on Philomena.

"I've given Mrs Dovetail something to speed her recovery," he said, looking mightily

pleased with himself. "God willing, the good woman will be as right as rain in a day or

two."

Mary put an arm around Lassa's shoulders. "There, what did I tell you?" she said. "She's going to be fine!"

Lassa let out a long sigh. "That's terrific news!"

She would be going home in two days!

She excused herself from the table and ran up the stairs two steps at a time in her

excitement. The Professor was going to be alright!

Everything was going to be alright!

She bounded into Philomena's room, beaming with joy.

"I've just been speaking with the doctor, Prof – " her voice broke off and her eyes

widened in shock. A small, strangulated sound escaped her mouth as it fell open in horror at

the sight before her.

Philomena lay flat on her back on the bed, her arms rigid at her sides. They were exposed

from her shoulders to the tips of her fingers and they were covered in thick, black, sausage-shaped creatures. They were on her temples and the cheeks of her face too. Lassa counted at

least thirty of them in all, ugly and slug-like, each one sucking silently at the Professor's

flesh.

"They're leeches," Philomena croaked, her face distorted with a fusion of revulsion and

fear. "I was asleep. When I awoke, the doctor was leaning over me with a leech jar. I was

too shocked to speak, let alone move. I couldn't stop him."

"I – I – I don't understand," Lassa said with a shake of her head.

"He said that my arms and legs are badly swollen and that the quickest

way to draw out the inflammation was to apply these blood-letting leeches. He said I will get

better much quicker if I allow them to feed on me."

Lassa's stomach churned with nausea.

Philomena's face crumpled. "They're on my legs too," she whimpered, not daring to

move.

Lassa guardedly pulled back the covers to reveal tens more of the repulsive little critters

and she recoiled in disgust, backing away.

"Ew!" she said, pulling a face.

"Will you – "

Pre-empting what the Professor was going to ask her to do, Lassa cried out.

"No way!" I'm not touching them!"

"Please!" Philomena beseeched her.

"But – I – " Lassa began to protest.

"Buckles and bootlaces! Can't you see I haven't the energy to remove them myself? I would if I could. Besides – ” Her voice broke away. She was embarrassed to say what came

next. “I couldn’t bear to touch them.”

Lassa moved forward and took a deep breath.

This just wasn’t her day.

Chapter Six

A Visit to Urton Hall

It took Lassa an hour to detach all the leeches and a further hour for Philomena to stop

bleeding. Although Philomena's temper did not improve after their removal, Lassa thanked

her lucky stars that she was clearly on the mend and that soon the two of them would be on their way home.

It was Monday morning. The rain had stopped and the sun was shining, though the

temperature was still very cool. After breakfast of horse-corn bread and eggs, Mary and

Lydia asked Lassa if she wanted to accompany them to Dr Calder's house. They wanted to

take his convalescing sister Clarissa a posy of flowers. Lassa had accepted their invitation at

once. She was keen to hear more of the highwayman and hoped that Clarissa would be well

enough and willing enough to speak of her encounter with him.

Dr Calder lived in a charming, secluded timber framed cottage to the north of the village.

It was flanked by apple trees and there was a pretty stone well in the garden, surrounded by a

fragrant lavender bed, together with foxgloves and hollyhocks.

Mary's knock on the panelled wooden door quickly fetched Dr Calder's

housemaid Nelly, who had sat with Philomena for a time the day before. She asked them to

wait in the hall so that she could first advise Dr Calder of their arrival, then motioned

them into the drawing room, where they found Dr Calder seated in his favourite gilded wood

armchair.

Dr Calder rose immediately to his feet upon seeing them and motioned them to take a seat

on a most attractive green velvet couch. Lassa recalled seeing one almost exactly like it on

The Antiques Roadshow, one of Pops' favourite TV shows. It had a serpentine shaped back,

scrolled out arms and six elegant cabriole legs, and was in keeping with the rest of the

furniture in the room, which was equally as stylish and as tasteful for the period.

"We wanted to call in on your sister, to see how she is fairing after yesterday's ordeal and

to give her our best regards," Mary said, looking - and feeling - a little ill at ease in such

opulent surroundings.

"That is very kind of you, Mary," said the doctor. "She and Henry are taking in the

morning air at the moment, but they will be back presently."

There was an embarrassed silence, and then Lydia spoke. "We have brought her flowers,"

she said.

"How very kind," said the doctor.

Another embarrassed silence.

"Perhaps we should leave." Mary said, levering herself up from the low couch.

"I wouldn't hear of it!" said Dr Calder.

Mary smoothed her dress and petticoats behind and under her as she retook her seat. She

gave a nervous little cough.

All of a sudden the door to the drawing room was pushed open and in stepped a

distinguished looking gentleman wearing a plain, tightly fitted coat and breeches. He was a

tall man of thin build with dark hair flecked with specks of grey, heavy looking eyebrows and

a prominent nose. He was closely followed by a woman of mid to late thirties in age wearing

a false-rumped robe. Her hair was piled high on her head and draped with a scarf.

Dr Calder rose from his seat, as did Mary, Lydia and Lassa.

"Ah, Henry. Clarissa," he said fondly. "May I introduce you to my good friend, Mrs Mary

Menzies, and her daughter Lydia. And this young lady – " - he gesticulated towards Lassa –

" – is their friend Miss Lassa Hope. She and her aunt were held up by Dan Dandy, just as

you were."

In an instant Clarissa dropped heavily into an elbow chair. She began to shake all over and

her face drained of colour. She flapped at her face with her hand. "Oh my Lord, do not talk

to me of that scoundrel!"

Dr Calder called for Nelly to fetch some water.

Henry began to fuss around his wife, loosening the scarf about her head.

"Clarissa, do not upset yourself," he said, laying a calming hand upon her knee.

"I just cannot bear to think of him," she managed to say after a few minutes, the tears

welling in her eyes. "And yet I cannot get his face out of my head!"

"Try to relax, Clarissa," Dr Calder fretted. "Henry is right, you mustn't upset yourself.

You will make yourself ill." He shook his head lamentably. "Dan Dandy has a lot to answer

for!" he declared, straightening up. "There were two hold ups in April of last year – another

in May – then Joseph Cruickshank was stopped in June – the Robottoms in July – Tobias and

Elsbeth Boothman in August – Sir John Lindsay in September – " - he stopped for breath -

"- the list goes on and on. Where, when and how will it all end?"

Mary handed Clarissa a lace handkerchief.

"Did you get a good look at his face then Mrs Fairweather?" she asked.

Clarissa dabbed at her eyes and gave an unladylike, derisory snort of laughter.

"No," she said at length, looking at them all in turn, her eyes finally coming to rest on

Lassa. “He made sure that I wouldn’t recognise him again. The coward wore a black eye mask and neck-chief about his face. All I could see was the evil in his eyes.”

A knock on the door heralded the return of Nelly, who walked in carrying a silver tray upon which sat a fluted jug of water and six tumblers. She lay the tray down to rest on an oak canopy dresser and left the room.

Dr Calder poured everyone a drink and they all retook their seats. To Lassa the cool, clear liquid tasted peculiar without the chemical and disinfection treatments to which she had become accustomed. She didn’t think it tasted particularly bad, just different, and she sipped at it nervously, wondering all the while if there was a chance it would make her ill.

“There was something though – ” Clarissa’s voice trailed off and her eyes grew narrow in sudden recollection.

"What? Clarissa, do tell us," Dr Calder prompted.

"The highwayman – Dan Dandy – he had a scar on his pistol finger," she declared. She

paused for effect, apparently enjoying the attention, and raised a tumbler of water to her lips.

"A nasty looking one at that!" she added, pulling a face.

Lassa sat on the edge of the couch on tenterhooks. This was all so exciting! She was

caught up in an adventure so thrilling and action-packed that she thought it would make a

successful Hollywood movie.

"Now don't get carried away, Clarissa," her husband said hastily, rousing Lassa from her

daydreaming.

Clarissa stared at him with steely determination.

"It's true, Henry!" she said. "I remember it vividly. As he raised his left arm – " - she

emulated what would have been the highwayman's actions by lifting her arm to shoulder

level - " – I caught a good look at his finger on the trigger. A red scar ran to his knuckle."

Dr Calder swallowed the last of his water and stood up to return it onto the tray on the

dresser. "That was very observant, Clarissa. We must inform the parish constable at once."

"Parish constable?" Lassa probed.

Everyone gaped at her as though she was quite mad and Lassa immediately regretted

asking the question.

It was Dr Calder who eventually responded. "A parish constable is an officer responsible

for keeping law an order on a day to day basis. Our village has three," he told her bombastically. "Each parish constable is sworn into their role by magistrates in the

county."

"Oh," said Lassa, blushing hotly. She dared a glance at Mary and Lydia and found that

they were staring at her intently. "Well of course I knew that. It just slipped my mind. "

"Quite so," said Henry, unconvinced. He did not know what to make of the strange little

girl before him and thought she must be foreign.

The room fell silent.

"Well, we mustn't outstay our welcome," said Mary, finding her feet. Respectfully,

Dr Calder and Henry rose also. "Oh, I nearly forgot, these are for you, Mrs Fairweather."

She handed the posy of white flowers to Clarissa, who accepted them appreciatively.

"They're beautiful, Mrs Menzies, thank you," she said, sniffing at their lovely perfume.

Mary, Lydia and Lassa left Dr Calder's cottage, promising to drop by again before the

Fairweathers returned to their home in Cheadle.

"Parsnip soup for lunch," Mary announced as they began their walk home.

Lassa groaned inwardly. She'd had her fill of parsnip soup. She longed for a plate of

her grandmother's homemade beef stew and dumplings. She closed her eyes and salivated at

the thought, rubbing her hands in dreamy anticipation. When she reopened her eyes, she was

smiling and she found that Mary was looking at her, her face flushed with pleasure.

"I'm flattered, Lassa," she enthused. "I never knew you found my parsnip soup so

agreeable."

Lassa avoided Mary's eye.

"Yes, it's super, it really is," she said over-enthusiastically so as to compensate for her flat

out lie.

Mary took a side-step towards Lassa and winked. "Then you shall have a second helping,"

she whispered surreptitiously in her ear.

Lassa feigned a smile and thanked her through gritted teeth. Me and my big mouth, she

thought. She could have kicked herself.

*

When they came to the fork in the road, Mary went one way, towards home, and Lydia and

Lassa went the other, towards the village.

"Let's go and see my father in his smithy," said Lydia, steering Lassa through an adjoining field.

"Okay," said Lassa.

They proceeded to tramp across the field at speed. The going was muddy following the

heavy rain and it was necessary for them to lift their dresses so as to avid soiling their hems.

"It's not too far," Lydia announced, leaping a small creek bowered in pussy-willow buds.

"In fact it's just past this field."

They reached the edge of the field and ran down a gravely embankment towards a dirt

track, beside which thick grass grew, course and prickly, and as they passed by, canary-

yellow buttercups nodded to them in the breeze.

It wasn't long after that the dilapidated, crumbling smithy loomed large before them,

encircled within bramble tangles and tall grasses threading through briars.

The doors were wide open, and they found Moses hard at work within the moss-covered

stone wall confounds. He was wielding a ball peen hammer and his muscled body was

sweating profusely.

"Father!" Lydia called to him.

Moses squinted in the light, made dark by the smoke from the forge. "Lydia? Is that you,

my love?"

Lydia and Lassa moved further into the shop and immediately upon seeing them Moses

stepped forwards to greet them both with a smile, his face and arms sooty and sweaty.

"And to what do I owe this pleasure?" he asked, glad of the excuse to take a break.

"Do I need a reason to come and see you, father?"

"No, of course not," he said indulgently.

"We've just come from Dr Calder's," Lassa told him. "We spoke with Mr and Mrs

Fairweather."

"Mrs Fairweather said that Dan Dandy has a scar on his trigger finger," Lydia said

excitedly.

"Is that so?" said Moses, raising a black powdered eyebrow in enquiry.

"Yes, and the most evil eyes she ever did see!" she went on with exaggeration.

Moses chuckled. "I doubt if anyone would recognise him in a crowd with a description

like that," he said with a humorous glint in his eye. He turned and faced the door of the shop

and raised his hammer, pointing it towards the dirt track outside.

"Fancy taking a walk with me, girls?" he asked, but he did not wait for their reply. He had already dropped his hammer and was removing his leather apron.

"Where are we going, father?" Lydia asked him.

"I want to call in on Mr Cruickshank." He wiped his hand on a rag. "He still owes me

three shillings."

Lydia and Lass exchanged nervous glances. They knew there was no love lost between

Moses and Joseph Cruickshank, and neither of them wanted to be caught in any crossfire.

But Moses would not be swayed.

"Come on," he said. "It won't take long. And I think Lassa would appreciate seeing the

gardens at Urton Hall."

*

Urton Hall was a most beautiful house situated adjacent to the river. It was built in 1695 of

local limestone and with its magnificent T-shaped plan and mullioned windows, Lassa

recognised it straight away.

In the 21st Century it existed as Urton Hall Hotel and Spa and had undergone extensive

restoration in the mid-1970s with the addition of an extra wing, which housed a Michelin

star-winning restaurant and bar. It was located just three miles from where Lassa lived with

her grandparents. Indeed, Nance had taken Lassa there as a three year old to enjoy the Easter

Bunny trail in its large grounds, landscaped by Calamity Brown with serpentine lakes and

undulating grass that ran straight up to the Hall, and Pops had celebrated his retirement as

city postmaster with a party in one of the elaborate function rooms. In the previous July,

Michael Bublé had performed at an outdoor concert in the gardens. The noise had carried

clearly to her bedroom and Lassa had been able to sing along to every song.

Whilst it had retained much of its natural beauty in Lassa's time, it in no way matched its

beauty now, in 1765, and Lassa could not prevent her mouth from falling open in awe upon

approach.

Observing Lassa's look of wonder, Moses said, "Grand, isn't it?"

"Oh yes," Lassa breathed, her eyes scanning the Hall's lovely frontage and the

Cruickshank Family Coat of Arms that adorned the exterior wall above the impressive front

door: Three bears, a fox and a blood red rose.

"Joseph Cruickshank's great grandfather commissioned the house to be built some seventy years ago, having made his fortune in London as a cornflour merchant," he said, sensing that

Lassa wanted to be filled in on its history. "No expense was spared. They say it took three

years to complete."

"With all his money and privilege you would have thought he'd be able to cover his debts

promptly, father," Lydia said tartly. It was evident from the tone in her voice that she

disliked Cruickshank intently. "While he enjoys deer and quail and pheasant, all washed

down with the finest wines, we eat parsnip soup."

With the mention of parsnip soup, Lassa suddenly found herself disliking Joseph

Cruickshank too.

"Yes, it's so unfair," Lassa said bitterly, returning to earlier thoughts of home-made beef

stew and dumplings, only this time her thoughts extended to a dessert too: A generous slice of banoffee pie with whipped cream. Her mouth watered.

Moses gave a loud snort. "Rumour has it that he has very little money now," he divulged.

"They say that it's all gone, that he's frittered it away in gambling dens in and around

London."

Lydia and Lassa looked shocked, but said nothing.

They discovered Joseph Cruickshank outside the stables standing with the stable-hand, a

young boy of no more than sixteen with a mop of curly brown hair. The boy was grooming

Cruickshank's white mare, whilst Cruickshank appeared to be lording it over him, telling him

in thunderous tones to do it this way, to do it that way; to do it quicker, to do it better.

Cruickshank did not notice Moses, Lydia and Lassa until they were upon him.

"Menzies," he acknowledged with a curt nod of his head.

Moses returned the gesture and respectfully tipped his hat.

"I've come for the three shillings you owe me, Mr Cruickshank sir," he said tersely.

A brief look of consternation flashed across Cruickshank's face.

"I don't think it pertinent to discuss this matter in front of – " – he shot Lydia and Lassa a

scathing look – " – <u>ladies</u>. Do you?" he asked, his blue eyes shadowed with annoyance.

Moses nodded and moved away towards Urton Hall. Cruickshank followed after him

stiffly.

"You're not the first to call by this week demanding payment for services rendered," the

stable-hand said in a low voice as he continued to groom the mare. He whistled softly to her

between his teeth as he brushed her, and she huffed at him through her nostrils, stirring restlessly. "He owes the cooper two pennies too."

Lassa reached out to stroke the mare's mane.

"You're a beauty, aren't you?" she whispered, and the mare whickered, nodding her white

head as though in agreement.

"Aye. there's no finer mare than White Lightning, not in all of England," the stable-hand

concurred. He passed his hand gently across her head and muzzle and she thrust her nose

into the hollow of his hand. "Groom her every day, I do, but I never wash her.

Mr Cruickshank likes to do that himself. I don't think he trusts me to do it properly; he likes

her to look immaculately white at all times."

Lydia and Lassa looked across at the Hall, where conversation between Cruickshank and

Moses was becoming progressively more and more heated, their loud voices carrying easily

in the breeze.

The stable door, which had been ajar, suddenly flew open in a gust of wind. Startled,

Lydia and Lassa averted their gaze from the two warring men and returned their attentions to

the stable-hand.

"Do you want to see something amazing?" he said to them in a whisper.

Lydia and Lassa nodded mutely.

"Then follow me."

He drew them into the stable. Inside, lying on a thin bed of straw was a new born foal, its

conker-coloured mother at its side, licking at its legs and under-belly.

"Oh wow!" Lassa exclaimed in delight.

“How lovely!” said Lydia, dropping to her knees in front of the foal.

The foal staggered unsteadily to its feet, its mouth blindly rooting for its mothers milk.

Lydia and Lassa oohed and ahhed in unsion.

“He was born this morning. I delivered him myself,” the stable-hand said, beaming with

pride.

A slim black cat ventured into the stable and made her delicate way across to the stable-

hand to twine her lithe body around his booted legs. The stable-hand reached down to pick

her up and she purred, nuzzling herself into the crook of his arm.

“And this is Midnight,” he said, rubbing her fondly under the chin.

Just then the stable door rattled open and Cruickshank appeared.

“Isaac!” he boomed, his face purple with fury.

Taken aback, the cat jumped from Isaac's arms and she scarpered outside, crashing into a

bucket of soot wash as she went.

Lydia rose to her feet slowly and straightened her dress.

"Isaac, fetch me my quill!" he demanded.

The stable-hand scurried off, looking alarmed and frightened.

With a brusque wave of his hand, Cruickshank gestured Lydia and Lassa out of the stable.

"You shouldn't be in here," he said abruptly.

"We did no harm, sir," Lassa said.

Cruickshank scowled as he drew the stable doors closed behind them.

"That's as maybe," he said. "But the foal needs time to familiarise himself to the stable,

and the mare needs her rest."

The girls found Moses standing outside. He was wringing his tricorn hat in his hands in agitation, his eyes fixed on his scowling antagonist.

The stable-hand returned then, puffing and red-faced, holding a feather quill, a vial of ink

and a rolled sheet of parchment. Cruickshank snatched them from him without thanks and

instructed him to turn around.

"I may not be in a position to pay you now, Menzies," he said, taking up the quill with his

left hand. "But if I commit the debt to parchment, it will act as a promissory note." He used

Isaac's back to lean on as he scribed. "Then you can call upon the debt at some later date."

He handed the parchment to Moses, who, not being able to read, regarded the

incomprehensible mass of letters with disdain.

"Oh can't you read, Menzies?" Cruickshank asked with an air of condescension.

Anger flashed in Moses' dark brown eyes.

"Whether I can read or not is beside the point," he growled. "This is worthless to me." He

screwed up the parchment and threw it onto the ground. "I need to feed my family now, not

at some later date."

Lydia and Lassa gave a sharp intake of breath. Isaac gawped.

A moment's ominous silence ensued.

"Come, girls," Moses said at last, donning his crumpled hat.

He marched off without another word, muttering and snarling under his breath. Lydia and

Lassa bade Isaac farewell and followed after him, tripping over themselves in their attempt to

keep with his large strides. They dared not open their mouths for the whole journey home.

Moses was in no mood for conversation.

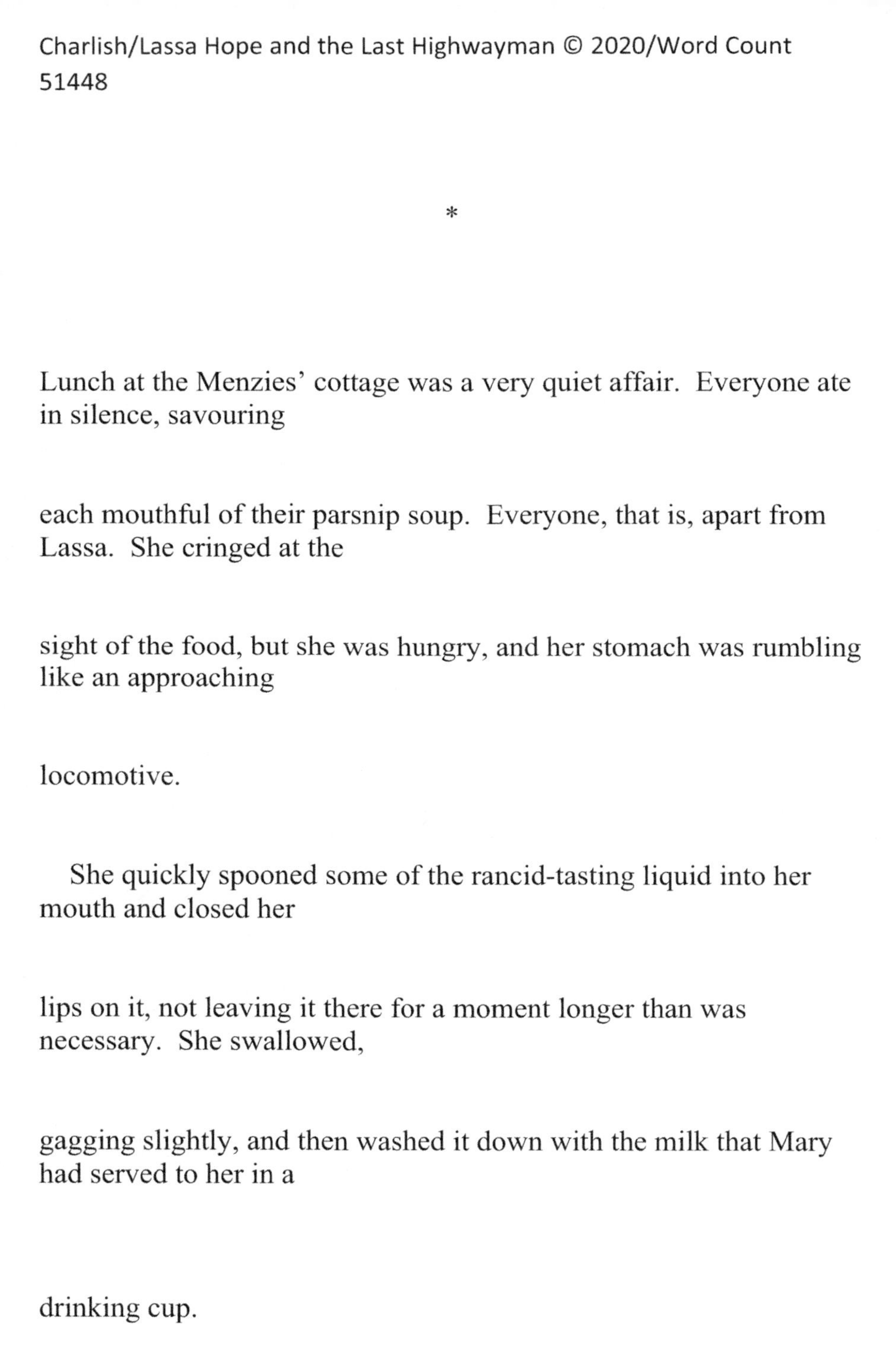

*

Lunch at the Menzies' cottage was a very quiet affair. Everyone ate in silence, savouring

each mouthful of their parsnip soup. Everyone, that is, apart from Lassa. She cringed at the

sight of the food, but she was hungry, and her stomach was rumbling like an approaching

locomotive.

She quickly spooned some of the rancid-tasting liquid into her mouth and closed her

lips on it, not leaving it there for a moment longer than was necessary. She swallowed,

gagging slightly, and then washed it down with the milk that Mary had served to her in a

drinking cup.

If I ever see a parsnip again it will be too soon, she thought to herself as she finally

emptied the bowl.

After lunch Lassa was left alone in the house with Philomena, who was now able to sit up

in bed quite comfortably.

Moses had returned to the blacksmith's shop. He had promised to repair the Fairweathers'

carriage, which had lost a wheel in the hold up the day before, having been forced to a

sudden and abrupt halt.

Mary had strolled into the village with the twins to buy a rabbit for supper and Lydia and

Esme had gone to the stream to wash their clothes with a soap made from fat and ashes.

Lassa recounted the day's events to Philomena, who by now was feeing thoroughly bored

and fed up. The bruising and swelling about her face and arms was beginning to go down and she had even managed to get out of bed briefly to use the toilet – a hole in the open

ground over a cesspit in the backyard. That, and the arrival of more parsnip soup at

lunchtime had done little to improve Philomena's rotten mood. The image of those leeches

glued to her naked body would stay with her for a long, long time.

"Dr Calder's home was lovely, Professor," Lassa said, sitting cross-legged on the edge of

Philomena's bed. "It was full of beautiful furniture, the likes of which I've only ever seen on

The Antiques Roadshow."

"Mmm, I bet it would fetch a pretty penny back in the 21st Century," Philomena remarked.

Back in the 21st Century.

Lassa gave a heavy sigh. It seemed so long ago that she'd last eaten normal foods: Crisps and chocolates and microwaveable ready meals laden with E numbers, additives and

colourings; and even longer that she had breathed air polluted not with the stench of parsnip

soup, foul-smelling trades and poor sanitation, but with diesel fumes and industry smoke

emissions.

Lassa sighed again.

Oh how she missed home.

Chapter Seven

Stand and Deliver

Before long Philomena fell asleep and Lassa took her leave of the room and went downstairs.

Moses was still at the smithy and Lydia and Esme were still at the stream. But Mary and

the twins had returned from the village with a small rabbit and were busy skinning and

gutting it in the kitchen in preparation for supper later that afternoon.

"Ah, Lassa," Mary said when she saw her. She was red faced and flustered and her apron

and hands were stained red with blood. "I have some rabbit innards for the cat that lives at

the smithy. Will you take them to Moses for me please?" Lydia's not back yet and I do not want them here, rotting. They will begin to smell before too long and they will attract flies."

Lassa felt nervous. She had not yet braved 18th Century England on her own, she had

always been with somebody else, like Lydia, Jacob or the Professor. But she had pushed

herself through many comfort zones in recent days; pushing herself through one more wasn't

likely to kill her.

She swallowed hard.

"Um, erm I suppose so," she floundered.

Mary smiled thankfully and her shoulders relaxed to drop visibly.

"Good. Here, take them." She passed Lassa a small parcel tied up with string. "And tell

Moses to be home before nightfall."

Lassa took a slow walk to the smithy. The weather was light and breezy and the stroll was a pleasant one. A carriage passed her by on the dirt track and its rider doffed his hat in

greeting. It was a million miles away from her 21st Century hometown, where cars and trucks

hooted their horns and where road rage was commonplace.

When she reached the smithy, she saw Moses in the glow of the forge, leather-aproned and

sweating, wiping his brow with the back of his hand.

"Mr Menzies?" Lassa said.

Moses straightened up and turned. He was clenching a hammer in his hand and looked

dead beat.

"Lassa?" he said, surprised. "Two visits in one day?"

Lassa moved forward, her eyes everywhere.

It was a huge shop, the floor space needing to be large to hold the wagons, ploughs and horses, although currently there were only two wagons and the one plough, and there were no

horses.

There was a workbench, a water drum, an anvil, a tool table, a forge and a coal bin.

Horseshoe racks hung on the clay walls, alongside racks for the iron and steel rods, and the

concrete floors about the forge and anvil were packed in soil.

"Mrs Menzies asked me to give you this. It's rabbit innards," Lassa said, handing over the

parcel. "For the cat," she explained at his quizzical look.

"Thank you," he said, placing the parcel on the bench.

"Mrs Menzies also said to tell you to be home before nightfall," she said. "May I stay with

you until then?"

"Of course," Moses replied with a nod.

He took up his tongs and thrust them into the forge. Seconds later he pulled out a length of

glowing, white iron.

Lassa stood, fascinated, watching in awe as he hammered the iron hard to weld and shape

it.

There was a knock at the door and Moses dipped the heated iron into the water drum and it

sizzled, steam rising.

"Come!" he instructed.

A dapper looking gentleman appeared, tall and thin-lipped, holding the reins of a robust

shire horse. He guided the beautiful beast into the smithy and passed the reins to Moses, who

stepped forward.

"He needs shoeing," he said.

"Not a problem, Mr Newman, sir," said Moses.

There was a ringing clang of hammer against anvil as Moses set to work and chips of hot

metal flew under the heavy blows. He pounded the hammer on the metal in rhythmic, expert

flow, and then smited it, shaping it until it cooled.

It was evident that he had shod horses for many, many years and Lassa marvelled at his

skill.

Moses applied the shoe to the horse's hoof to check for size, then returned it to the heat,

hammering on the anvil repeatedly, the sparks flying up and fading. And then, finally,

having created the perfect horseshoe, he shod the horse, and an acrid smell of burning hoof

filled the smithy and Lassa's nostrils.

He repeated the process three more times, then Mr Newman paid up – eight pennies, two for each shoe – mounted his shire and left.

Job done, Moses dragged a rag across his sweat-slicked forehead and rubbed his hands

down his apron.

"If only they all paid up on time," he said, setting his hammer down on the workbench.

At that precise moment, they heard the hoof-beats of an approaching horse – clip-clop-clip-

clop-clip-clop – and Moses downed his hammer and went outside to meet his next customer.

Lassa followed silently after him.

It was Joseph Cruickshank astride his beautiful white coated mare, White Lightning. He

was moving around in a large circle, but upon seeing Moses he reigned her to a halt. He did

not dismount.

Moses flashed him a hostile look, but said nothing.

Lassa remained at the smithy door, conscious of the oppressive atmosphere. She too said

nothing.

It was Joseph Cruickshank who spoke first, looking down at Moses from the snuffling,

sixteen-hands-high horse.

"She has lost a shoe on her hind leg, Menzies," he said crisply. "I was hacking 'cross

country when it happened. It's the mud left from the rains that does it. The soft ground does

not agree with her."

Moses smiled up at him humourlessly. Lassa held her breath and gripped on to the smithy

door, her body tense with an ominous sense of foreboding.

"Hand over the three shillings you owe me and I'll shoe your mare," Moses said in a measured voice. "Don't and I won't, that's how it is."

From the tone of Moses' voice Joseph Cruickshank was left in no doubt that he meant

every word.

"Do you mean to say that you won't shoe my mare unless I first settle my debt?"

"That, sir, is exactly what I mean to say," replied Moses levelly.

Cruickshank looked as though he was going to explode, but he quickly regained his poise.

He coaxed the mare to take a side step towards Moses and placed his tapering leather riding

crop under Moses' chin to lift it ever so slightly. Moses looked up at him unblinkingly, his

fists clenched at his sides.

"I am a very influential and powerful man, Menzies," he said coolly, raising his riding crop higher so that Moses was forced to crane his neck up to look up at him. "You would do well

to remember that. I don't suggest that you make an enemy of me. I have a great deal of

friends and you are not the only farrier in these parts."

He ran the riding crop up from under Moses' chin and along the side of his face, resting it

menacingly upon his cheekbone. To his credit, Moses stood his ground and did not flinch.

"So..." Cruickshank continued, his voice cool and clipped. "With that said, what say

you re-consider shoeing my mare?" He tapped the crop on Moses' cheek, not once, but

twice. "Well?" he smirked.

From where she stood just outside the smithy, still gripping steadfastly onto the outer

wooden door, Lassa's heart beat a violent tattoo inside her ribcage. Silently she willed Moses

not to yield to his tormentor.

And then it hit her. Like a bolt from the blue.

Not once had she had the guts to make a stand with her own tormentor, Clare Fox. Lassa

had always played the victim. She had never retaliated or tried to defend herself in any way,

either physically or verbally, and consequently Clare Fox had continued to pick on her,

forever considering her to be an easy target.

Ignoring bullies just didn't work. The problem would never go away unless the problem

was taken in hand. It dawned on Lassa that bullies have their own problems, problems that

make them feel upset and angry, and often the only way for them to feel better about

themselves is to pick on others.

Joseph Cruickshank's problems were financial. He had gambling debts and in all probability, he would have creditors and gambling partners leaning on him to pay up,

threatening him, making him feel small and vulnerable. He was just transferring that feeling

of hopelessness and misery on to Moses and no doubt on to other men of an equally low

social standing. It would almost certainly help to make him feel superior, for a

time at least.

Moses snatched the riding crop from Joseph Cruickshank's hand and Lassa silently

applauded him.

"You don't unnerve me, Cruickshank," he said gruffly, but a twitch to the side of his

mouth belied his words. Lassa could tell that he was beginning to get edgy.

A fine misty drizzle began to fall and Cruickshank glanced up at the steel grey clouds that loomed over. He cursed under his breath, a blasphemous curse that would have earned him a

day in the stocks had it been heard by anyone other than Moses Menzies, the impoverished

blacksmith.

As the rain began to fall more fervently, it skidded off the bald dome at the front of

Cruickshank's head and slicked the brown curls at the back of his scalp.

"Is that so?" he said irritably and through gritted teeth.

He was clearly not impressed by Moses' refusal to be intimidated and Lassa supposed he

was not accustomed to people not doing what he asked or demanded of them.

"It is," said Moses with a steely determination not to be bettered. He handed the riding

crop back to Joseph Cruickshank. "Like you say, I'm not the only farrier in these parts. I would prefer it if you took your business to one of them. Consider your debt paid. I neither

want nor need your money."

Cruickshank nudged his mount and she lifted her head and tail high. He coaxed her into a

piaffe and she trotted smartly in place, feet prancing. He manoeuvred her slowly forward

towards Moses, placing the stirrup and his boot until it was almost in contact with his face.

"You will live to regret this, Menzies," he spat.

He commanded his mare forward and kicked his heels roughly into her flanks. She broke

off at once into a gallop. And then they were gone.

Lassa heaved a huge sigh of relief. Standing beside her, Moses drew a long and ragged

breath.

"Well done!" she beamed up at him. "You stood firm." She gave him an impulsive hug.

"I'm so proud of you."

Humbled, Moses returned the hug.

"He won't try to browbeat you again," Lassa continued with a beatific smile.

Moses gave a ghost of a smile.

"I wouldn't be so sure of that, Lassa," he said sagely.

He walked back into the smithy, took up his hammer and began to pound arduously at a

sheet of metal.

For the next two hours Lassa watched him as he vented his pent up anger and frustration,

swinging his hammer and slamming it down repeatedly, rivers of sweat pouring off him. She

allowed him this time to burn off the ball of nervous energy that welled inside him, before

reminding him that Mary wanted him home before nightfall.

"We're having rabbit," she said at his apparent reluctance to lay down his hammer.

"My favourite," he said, but still he did not stop work.

After a few moments Lassa stepped forward to place a tentative hand on his right arm,

preventing him from raising the hammer again.

"Mr Menzies, it's time to go home," she said, removing the hammer from his hands. She

lay it on the workbench and there was a resounding dull sound of metal against wood. "Mrs

Menzies will be getting anxious. And the rabbit will be getting cold."

Moses was surprised at Lassa's forthrightness. She seemed older than thirteen somehow,

older than Lydia in many ways, and she commanded respect in spite of her tender age.

Moses realised that he knew very little about her and he wondered if she could be of noble

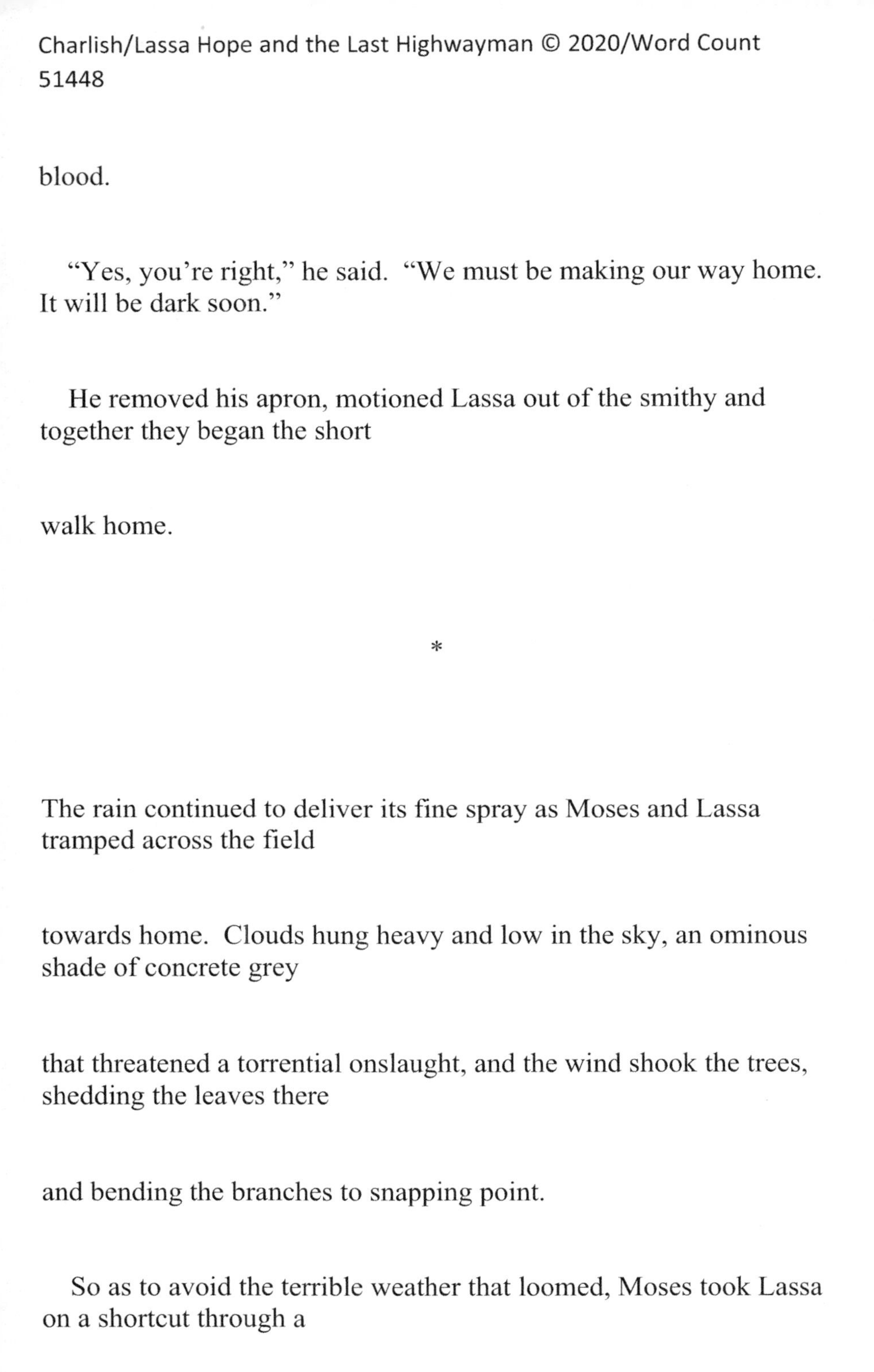

blood.

"Yes, you're right," he said. "We must be making our way home. It will be dark soon."

He removed his apron, motioned Lassa out of the smithy and together they began the short

walk home.

*

The rain continued to deliver its fine spray as Moses and Lassa tramped across the field

towards home. Clouds hung heavy and low in the sky, an ominous shade of concrete grey

that threatened a torrential onslaught, and the wind shook the trees, shedding the leaves there

and bending the branches to snapping point.

So as to avoid the terrible weather that loomed, Moses took Lassa on a shortcut through a spinney, pointing out anything and everything that he thought may have been of interest to

her.

Lassa had been on a nature trail before, but nothing compared to this. She was seeing the

English countryside at its very best, untouched by man, and in its rawest, most natural form.

When she closed her eyes she could smell the hollyhocks, delphiniums, lavender,

campanulas and gorse. She could hear the song of the lark and the call of the peregrine to its

mate high in the sky above.

It was an experience completely untainted by man's unquenchable thirst for industrial,

commercial and technological progress, where flowers, vegetables and fauna grew without

the use of pesticides, additives, growth hormones and the scientific interference of genetic modification.

It was a truly magical place, in spite of the rain and the cold, and Lassa felt heady and at

peace with the world.

Just before they reached the grass verge at the end of the field, Lassa stumbled over a tree

root and she fell to her knees on the ground. She grazed her hands, but was otherwise

unhurt. Moses crouched beside her and she drew a sharp intake of breath.

"That looks sore," he said.

Without warning they heard a scream, a high-pitched blood curdling scream coming from

the road. At once Moses sensed danger.

"Shh…" he instructed Lassa in a whisper, placing a finger over her lips as she went to speak. he placed a firm, preventative hand on her shoulder. "Don't say a word. Not. One.

Single. Word."

Between the end of the field and the road there was a natural trench; a long, narrow, yet

deep depression in the ground that ran for some twenty five feet or more. Moses regarded it

pensively, chewing on his bottom lip.

"We'll be hidden from view in there," he said in a low voice. "We'll be safe."

Without further ado he took a hold of Lassa's hand and together they moved slowly

forward on their haunches to slide silently inside the trench. It was cold, cramped and

muddy. The recent heavy rains had created a channel of thick, brown sludge, and Moses and

Lassa found themselves up to their knees in it. Insects and worms crawled and wriggled alongside them, but Lassa cared not for them. She was more interested in what was

happening over the other side of the trench, on the road that led from the village.

Breathless and wide eyed with fear, Lassa and Moses hauled themselves up and peered

nervously over the edge.

The sight that greeted them was one that made their blood run cold.

It was Dan Dandy, mounted upon his beautiful black and white horse. He was wielding a

pistol.

And it was pointed at somebody's head.

*

Dan Dandy was wearing his trademark leather eye mask and black leather neckerchief, the latter having been tied loosely at the back of his head in a single knot to leave only his eyes

visible.

Evil eyes.

Clarissa Fairweather had been right about that.

Two cruel, heartless narrow slits staring at the occupant of the carriage with a disarming

lack of emotion.

They were blue, Lassa observed. A piercing blue that chilled her to the bone and sent

shivers down her spine.

"Do as I ask and nobody will get hurt!" Dan Dandy was heard to say, his voice muffled

and indistinguishable through the neckerchief.

Lassa eyed the broad-shouldered coachman sitting in the middle of the box high up in the carriage. He was stony-faced and still. He was in his early fifties with iron grey hair and

wore a dull green livery with white trim. He was clinging onto the horses' reins as though

his very life depended upon it. And it may well have done. His knuckles were pale, the

skin stretched taut across the back of his hands, and his eyes were wide open in fear.

His passenger was a good ten years older. He was bald to the middle of his head, while

long grey hair fell over the neck of his frock coat in large curls. His shoulders heaved as he

gulped in air in desperate, terrified mouthfuls.

Dan Dandy barked an order for the coachman and his passenger to climb down from the

carriage. The pair of them quickly obliged, their arms raised in the air in deference to the

pistol being waved at them. Their whole bodies shook. As the passenger moved across to the rear of the carriage, he dropped his hands to his face and began to sob convulsively,

pleading with the highwayman to spare his life.

"Please – don't – don't kill me – " - he begged, edging ever so slowly backwards - " – I

have money. Take it, take everything!"

His clothes were much too large for him and appeared to have been made for him at a time

when he was much more stout. His breeches were not held up by braces and he could not

walk five paces without having to pull them up and re-adjust them.

"Shut up!" Dan Dandy shouted.

He pulled hard on his horse's reins and fired a warning shot from his pistol. The horse

whinnied loudly and reared up to stand on its hind legs before standing down again. Its

barrel-chest and haunches bespoke a tremendous strength. Its black nostrils flared open and closed in wrath, ears pricked, mane bristling, tossing its head from side to side with a

haughty indignation. It truly was a magnificent beast and Lassa considered it to be a shame

that it was being used to aid and abet such a horrible criminal venture as this.

Dan Dandy brought the horse under control with a click of his tongue and a short, sharp

"Whoa!" His dark, full length coat had fallen open in the furore and his white, ruff-coloured

shirt had become visible beneath, as had the flintlock pistols that he wore strapped across his

chest in tan leather pouches at either side of his hip, one for powder, one for bullets.

From inside the trench Moses and Lassa looked on helplessly. Their legs were beginning

to cramp up in their close confines, pain seizing at their muscles, and their bodies were

trembling with fright and the cold.

Lassa's heart was hammering against her chest wall so loud and so fast that she feared Dan

Dandy would be able to hear it.

"I'm scared," she whispered to Moses.

Moses slid an arm around her shoulders and pulled her close.

"Just be quiet and everything will be fine," he assured her.

They turned back to look back at the events unfolding on the road. Dan Dandy was now

demanding that the coachman turn out his pockets.

The coachman dutifully did as he was asked They were empty, save for a few pennies and

a small, half-eaten meat pie . Dan Dandy discarded the pie and plopped the coins into a

purpose-made leather pouch strapped to the side of his saddle. His evil eyes flashed steely

blue.

"Is this all you carry?" he demanded hoarsely.

The coachman nodded without a sound.

Dan Dandy dismounted his horse and tethered its reins to a fence at the side of the road.

He pulled a blade from his hip-belt and approached the coach. With a quick slash, he cut the

harness and smacked hard on each of the two horses' hides. The horses galloped off at speed.

"What have you done?" the coachman cried out in alarm. "I cannot drive further without

the horses!"

"Precisely," Dandy said with a smile in his voice. He pointed his pistol at the coachman's

head and cocked it.

"Do you take issue with that, sir?"

The colour drained from the coachman's face as he stared down the barrel of the pistol.

"No, sir, I don't," he said, his voice all of a quiver, his hands raised in the air in

submission.

Dandy lowered his weapon. "I thought not," he said with a short laugh.

He moved across to the whimpering passenger, his pistol still cocked and ready to fire.

"And you, sir, what do you have for me?" he asked.

The passenger, his face stricken, cowered away from the barrel of the gun, which was

poised just an inch or so from his temple.

"You can have everything I have, sir, just please – please don't – don't shoot!" He

covered his face with his hands, his voice rising to a whine. "Don't shoot me, I beg of you."

"Hand over your money!" Dandy demanded impatiently.

"Please – please – "

Dandy drew back his arm and pistol whipped him hard across the face, not once, but twice.

The passenger staggered backwards, bleeding profusely from his nose, and whimpered like a

newly born pup.

"Hand over your money NOW!" Dandy demanded again. "And your valuables too."

Moses and Lassa looked on, horrified, as the passenger handed over a jingling leather

pouch, a sterling silver watch and chain and two Keeper rings.

Then, out of the blue, the coachman struck Dandy on the back with a clenched fist and

made a grab for the pistol. To the two startled observers, still hidden deep inside the trench at

the edge of the field, what happened next seemed to unfold in slow motion.

Dan Dandy swung around swiftly and connected his knee to the coachman's stomach. The coachman doubled over and fell to the floor. As he moaned in pain, Dan Dandy ambled over

to his horse to stow away his booty in the pouch at the side of his saddle.

"Fancied yourself as the hero of the hour, did you?" He gave a nasty laugh, made safe his

pistol, then holstered it. "What a fool!"

Assisted by the still-bleeding passenger, the coachman staggered to his feet, swaggering

and swaying as though drunk on mead.

"You scoundrel!" the coachman spat.

"You will hang for this!" the passenger rasped. "I – um – I – "

Suddenly his words became inaudible as his face contorted in a mask of pain. He clutched

at his chest, his face white and clammy, his eyes wide and unblinking. And then he collapsed

to the ground, apparently lifeless.

The coachman fell to his knees at his side. "You've scared the man half to death! His

heart has all but given up in fright!"

He cried out, and with a bravery borne out of panic and fear, he lunged at the highwayman.

But he was no match for Dan Dandy, who was much younger, more lithe and supple. he

side-stepped at the right moment, and the coachman's flailing hands made contact not with

him, but with empty space, and he faltered, stumbling to the floor.

"You really do fancy yourself as the hero of the hour!" Dandy said. His voice was

monotone, yet it still conveyed sarcasm.

The coachman sprung hotly to his feet and swung an inarticulate fist at Dandy's head.

Predictably, it missed. Dandy struck him squarely under the jaw. The coachman whirled half

round and fell to the ground, out cold.

From inside the trench, Moses and Lassa gazed at the paralysed figure.

Something inside Moses snapped. "I must help him, Lassa. I must."

He made to leave, but Lassa laid a preventative hand on his shoulder.

"No, please – " Her eyes were pleading. "It's too dangerous!"

Moses regarded her levelly. "I must, Lassa, " he told her apologetically. "What kind of

man would I be if I just sat here in this ditch and didn't make a move to help. That coachman

out there might have a wife. Children."

"It would make you a safe man," Lassa said tartly.

But Moses would not be swayed. "I'm sorry," he whispered.

He hauled himself up and over the trench. And then was gone.

Lassa held her breath. She had never been so scared. She was on her knees in the mud and

they were shaking so much that she had to put her hands on her thighs to steady them. her

heart was in her mouth as she watched Moses creep up behind Dan Dandy, then grab him,

spinning him around.

"What the – ?" Dan Dandy was taken aback.

"It's high time somebody put an end to your fun and games," Moses said evenly, balling

his fists.

Dan Dandy gave a derisory snort. "And how do you suppose to do that, Menzies?"

"By doing this!"

Moses' fist made contact with Dandy's face.

Taken off guard, Dandy was momentarily unbalanced and he staggered backwards, slamming into the side of the carriage with a resounding thud.

Dandy's eyes glittered dangerously over his neckerchief.

"You'll regret that!" he spat.

He flew at Moses and the two of them tumbled to the floor, rolling about on the road, their

bodies tangled as one.

Lassa could only watch in horror as the two men continued to tussle, their hands tugging

and tearing at each other, their legs kicking, their teeth biting. She blinked hard, trying to

hold back a cascade of hysterical tears from flooding down her cheeks. She felt completely

powerless to help.

And then it was over.

Dandy rose to his feet.

Moses did not.

*

Dandy kicked at Moses' still body with the tip of his boot. Lassa thought he must be dead,

but then she heard him moan, a low moan, followed by a rattling of breath, and she knew that

he must have just been knocked unconscious.

There was a noise. In the distance. And it was drawing rapidly closer. Angry men, baying

dogs and a dozen pairs of pounding feet. All were approaching fast.

Lassa saw Dandy's evil eyes widen in alarm.

Just then a huge black rat appeared in the sludge inches in front of Lassa's knees. Her

body instantly froze in fear. She watched, eyes unblinking, as the rat scuttled towards her

and she suppressed a squeal as its thick, long tail, at least twice the size of its body, whipped past her nose to scurry further on down the trench.

When she looked up she saw Dandy riding down the road at great speed. His body was

sunk down low on the heaving back of his horse, his face buried in the flying black mane.

Moses was still lying prostrate on the road.

Only now he was wearing Dandy's tricorn hat, his neckerchief, leather eye-mask and

cloak, and the pistol had been placed in his hand.

Lassa swallowed hard.

To the angry men approaching, she knew exactly how this would look.

And it would not look good.

Chapter Eight

The Tricorn Hat

It wasn't long before the men of the village, having been alerted by the noise of pistol fire,

came upon the horseless carriage.

They unleashed their snapping, snarling dogs on approach, and Lassa watched as they

sniffed and salivated at the three bodies lying motionless on the ground.

The coachman was the first to stand. He appeared groggy and was rubbing his head as

though he could not quite recollect, or indeed believe, the events that had just passed.

The passenger, who had to be assisted, rose to his feet soon after. He was weak and

scared, and although visibly much improved, was taken directly to Dr Calder's cottage as a precaution.

The men then turned their attentions to Moses, slowly closing in on him until his still,

dishevelled body was completely surrounded.

After a few moments he began to stir and one of the men stepped forward to pull him

roughly to his knees, knocking the tricorn hat from his hat. Moses objected feebly, still dazed

and disorientated, as a second man unceremoniously ripped off the eye-mask and

neckerchief.

There was a collective shocked gasp when the crowd saw that it was Moses Menzies, the

village blacksmith, beneath the disguise.

"I can hardly believe my eyes!" declared one astounded man.

"Surely it can't be!" said another.

Moses was too muzzy-headed to comprehend the situation. He staggered to his feet, still

reeling from his scuffle with Dan Dandy, and wobbled forward. Lassa noticed to her alarm

that he was still holding the pistol.

The men backed quickly away, their voices a mixture of anger and fear.

"Put the pistol down, Menzies!" one man ordered boldly.

"You'll hang for this Menzies!" yelled another.

"You rotter!" cried a third.

Menzies followed their line of vision to the pistol in his hand.

"I – I don't understand," he uttered miserably, scratching and shaking his head. But as

soon as the words had left his mouth, his mind became less cloudy and he realised to his horror that Dan Dandy must have witched clothes and left the pistol in his hand to implicate

him in the robbery. At once Moses realised how things must appear to the men

standing fearfully before him. He knelt down slowly to place the pistol on the gravelled road.

"This isn't what it looks like, I – I – the highwayman – Dan Dandy – he – " Moses

spluttered desperately. "Please, it's a misunderstanding. I would never – "

One of the men kicked the pistol away, out of Moses' reach. A second man hauled him to

his feet, whilst a third grabbed his arm and forced it high up behind his back.

"You've got it all wrong!" Moses protested, wincing in pain.

But the men were not listening. In their minds, they had captured Dan Dandy, and they

wanted him brought to justice.

The last thing Lassa saw was the men dragging Moses away, back towards the village.

They were whooping and clapping, happy in their misplaced belief that they had brought an

end to the highwayman's reign of terror.

Lassa remained in the trench, trembling and afraid, for what seemed like a lifetime. Night

had long since fallen and the birds were beginning to return to their nests, twittering in the

trees overhead. The darkness had seemed to swallow all colour and the only light emanated

from the moon in the sky above, appearing as one long silver streak that fell across the

road.

Slowly, and with trepidation, Lassa struggled to haul herself out of the trench, clawing at

the muddy sides like a bear in a trap. Her face and hands were caked with sludge and her wet petticoats clung to her body like a second skin.

She was tired and her whole body ached, but she was anxious to get back to the Menzies'

cottage as fast as she possibly could.

Finding the strength from she knew not where, she took a bold step forward, grabbed the

hem of her dress and raised the heavy material to her knees to run home. Her heart was in

her mouth, its rapid beat resounding in her head and ears like a drum.

She had to get home, to Mary, to Lydia and the children.

*

When Lassa reached the Menzies' cottage, there was a carriage standing outside. Lassa

recognised the horses and the markings on the side at once: It belonged to Dr Calder.

Inside the cottage there was much wailing and beating of breasts. Mary was sat in Moses'

favourite chair by the fire in the sitting room, her body racked with sobs, and Lydia was stood

over her, howling as though she was in pain.

Dr Calder stood morosely in the corner, his hat in his hands, his head held low.

Thankfully, Esme and the twins were safely tucked up in bed, and had been for some time,

and so they were oblivious to the horrifying turn of events.

"Oh Lassa! Lassa!" Lydia cried, tears flowing unchecked down her cheeks. "Father has

been arrested!"

Lassa turned to Dr Calder sharply. "But Dr Calder he – "

Dr Calder prevented her from saying more with a raise of his hands. "Mr Menzies was taken by Captain Bywater and conveyed immediately to Newgate Prison," he said sullenly.

"In a week's time he will be tried – " - he paused to take a shaky breath - " – then

condemned, if found guilty, and - "

" - and then executed!" Mary finished with a howl. She dropped her head into her hands, a

cry of anguish bursting from within. "My Moses is not a highwayman, I tell you. That man is

incapable of anything that isn't anything but kind!"

"She's right, Dr Calder," Lassa blurted. "I was hiding in a ditch, close to the road. I saw it

happen, the whole thing. And Mr Menzies is not guilty."

Lassa recounted the afternoon's events, culminating with details of Moses' brawl with

Dandy, and how the latter had switched clothes and planted the pistol in Moses' hand to incriminate him.

"Is this true?" Dr Calder regarded Lassa through narrowed eyes.

"Yes! Yes! It's true! All of it, I swear!" Lassa said, frantic to be believed. "All Mr

Menzies did was try to help!"

Dr Calder gave a lamentable shake of his head. "Either way, they will never believe you.

You're a family friend. And a child," he added pointedly. "But this is indeed a very sorry

state of affairs. I pray that the truth will out and that justice prevails."

He replaced his hat, bid a civil farewell and left the cottage. The cottage door banged shut

heavily behind him to rattle noisily on its hinges.

Mary fell back in her chair. "They will hang my wonderful husband for something he did

not do," she said with a whisper, her prophetic words heralding more plaintive cries from

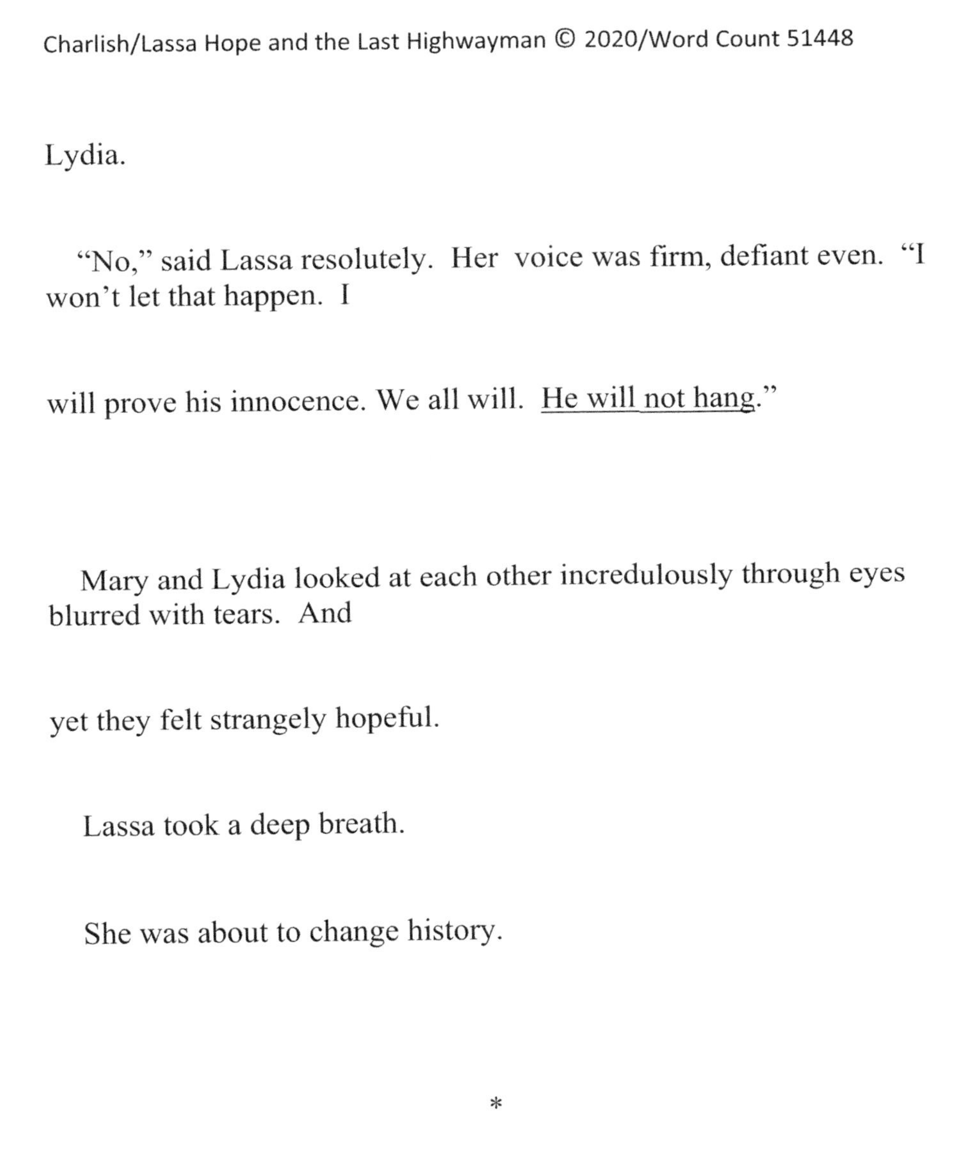

Lydia.

"No," said Lassa resolutely. Her voice was firm, defiant even. "I won't let that happen. I

will prove his innocence. We all will. He will not hang."

Mary and Lydia looked at each other incredulously through eyes blurred with tears. And

yet they felt strangely hopeful.

Lassa took a deep breath.

She was about to change history.

*

Philomena was sitting up in bed, her neck craned towards the bedroom door, her ears pricked.

"What's going on downstairs?" she asked when Lassa finally entered the room. "I can hear lots of shouting and crying. What a hullabaloo!"

Lassa sank down on the edge of the bed and burst into tears, worry washing through her

like a wave upon the shore.

"Oh Professor, something dreadful has happened," she said.

Philomena shuffled forward on the bed and reached out to stroke Lassa's red-brown hair.

"What is it, what has happened?"

"Mr Menzies has been arrested!" Lassa blarted.

Philomena stroked a stray strand of hair out of Lassa's eyes.

"Well, you knew this would happen, didn't you?" she said. "You knew from the school's

library that he was the last man to hang on Gibbet Hill. All the reference books confirmed

it."

"But he's an innocent man!" Lassa protested. He was stitched up, framed by the true

culprit, the cowardly – " She stopped suddenly, her eyes widening with recollection. "The

cowardly highwayman – Dan Dandy – he knew Mr Menzies!"

"How do you know that?" Philomena asked.

"Because he actually referred to him by name!"

The highwayman's muffled voice replayed in her mind. "And how do you suppose to do

that, Menzies?"

"I'm going to prove Mr Menzies is an innocent man, Professor. I will not allow him to die.

I believe that is the reason we are here, to save him from the gallows."

"I admire your spirit, Lassa, really I do. But you cannot change the past. There will be repercussions in our time, changes made that could affect our own timeline."

Lassa jumped to her feet. "I can change the past and I will," she said. "And as for

repercussions, it's a risk we need to take."

This wrong needs to be made right, Lassa thought to herself, if it's the very last thing I do.

*

The next morning before breakfast, Lassa and Lydia set off to Captain Bywater's residence at

the edge of the village. It was Mary who had suggested the idea. She had known the captain

since she was a little girl; they had often played together as children in the woods, and she

thought that maybe he would hear Lassa's story, see reason, and work to free her husband.

Lassa was not so sure that her word alone - the word of a child – would free Moses.

However, knowing as she did that Moses was innocent of all charges, she was also confident

that she would be able to find all the proof she needed to secure Moses' release from

Newgate Prison. And, to this end, she would do all that it took. Lydia, for her part, was

happy to help out in any way she could.

The young girls were pleasantly surprised when the captain agreed to meet with them. He

was a busy man, but he was also a virtuous one, and he was happily prepared to spare some

time to talk to the smithy's eldest daughter and her young friend, to hear what they had to

say, particularly if it had some bearing on the impending trial. He knew that Moses Menzies was a good man and he himself could scarcely believe Moses capable of being a

highwayman, so he was keen to learn more and to help if he could.

As Captain Bywater's housekeeper hastened the girls into his elaborately furnished sitting

room, Lassa felt as though she could physically breathe in the affluence and wealth that

oozed from its four walls. The captain himself was just as impressive. A handsome man with

dark hair tied at the nape, he wore a three quarter length blue velvet coat, breeches with gold

buttons and gold embroidered buttonholes. The large cuffs of his coat were pure silk and

matched his gold-frogged waistcoat. He resembled the men on the cover of the romantic

novels her grandmother read and for a brief moment, Lassa was distracted by the

reminder of her home and of her grandparents, who she dearly missed.

Captain Bywater bade his housekeeper to fetch some fresh milk and cake and smoothed his

coat tails to take a seat on a cushioned elbow chair. The two girls sat down before him,

sharing a plush red settee.

Lassa did not waste any time in reminding the influential naval officer of their reasons for

their visit.

"Mr Menzies is not a highwayman, sir," she said. "I was there. I saw it all. It was

somebody else. I don't know who, but I can tell you that it was not Mr Menzies."

"You were there? You saw it all?" Captain Bywater asked. It was meant as a rhetorical

question, but Lassa answered anyway.

"Yes, I was. And yes, I did, sir," she said. "I was hidden in a ditch, close to the road where the carriage was held up. Mr Menzies went to assist the coachman and his passenger,

but he was knocked unconscious in the struggle. That was when the highwayman switched

clothes with him – mask and all – to make it look as though Mr Menzies was the

highwayman." She shuddered. "And then he placed the pistol in Mr

Menzies' hand, incriminating him further still."

Captain Bywater paused for a moment and clasped his hands together at his chin, bringing

his two fingertips up to his lips as he pondered her words.

"You say you saw it all," he said thoughtfully. "Then you must have caught a glimpse of

the real perpetrator of the crime as he removed his mask and neckerchief to place them on Mr

Menzies."

Lassa felt herself redden.

"Well – no – I – I'm afraid I didn't," she revealed awkwardly. "I was looking down into

the ditch. At a rat – " She broke off, embarrassed. "I don't like rats, sir, and I didn't want it

crawling over me. When I looked up again, the highwayman had already fled on his horse."

There was a knock on the sitting room door and the housekeeper appeared with a tray.

"Mmmm," mused the captain as the housekeeper served them their milk. "If I am to

believe you, and I am not saying that I do – this all seems highly convenient - I will first need

proof that what you are saying is true. Do you have any?"

Lassa sipped at her milk. When she withdrew her drinking cup away from her mouth a

thin white line above her upper lip remained.

"Not at the moment," she said unhappily. "All I know for sure is that the highwayman knew Mr Menzies, since he spoke to him by name."

Lydia gestured to Lassa to wipe her mouth. Lassa did so.

"But lots of people know Mr Menzies," said the captain. "I can hardly arrest them all on

suspicion of being Dan Dandy, the notorious highwayman, now can I?" He lay his empty

drinking cup down on a low, mahogany table at his side. "Without a confession from the real

villain or proof – and by proof I mean conclusive evidence – I am afraid that I cannot help

you further." He looked across at Lassa, then at Lydia, before his eyes finally rested again on

Lassa. "I have a dozen or so respectable witnesses who are willing to testify that they saw

Moses Menzies dressed as a highwayman at the scene of a highway robbery than nearly cost

two men their lives. He will surely hang unless – "

" – unless we find proof." Lassa finished the sentence for him.

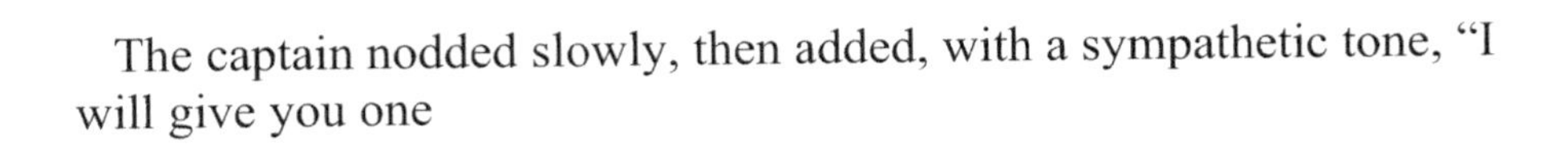

The captain nodded slowly, then added, with a sympathetic tone, "I will give you one week."

Lassa and Lydia rose to their feet.

"Thank you for your time, sir," they said, their voices hollow. They were grateful for that, if nothing else.

"You're welcome," Captain Bywater replied.

Dismissing his housekeeper, the captain himself escorted the girls out of the sitting room and through the hallway. At the front door he turned to them, his expression earnest and sincere.

"Before his apprehensive last night, I believed Menzies to be a good blacksmith – and an even better man," he said. "I hope you find your proof."

Lydia gave him a tremulous smile. "We will, sir," she said. "Together, Lassa and I will

find all the proof we need."

Just then Lassa spotted a tricorn hat sitting on a dark rosewood table that stood against the

wall.

"That's Dan Dandy's hat isn't it?" she ventured. It was a hunch more than a certainty.

"Yes," replied the captain. "It was retrieved at the scene of the robbery. The one

Mr Menzies was found wearing."

"May I look at it?"

The captain thought for a moment, eyeing Lassa warily, but then realising there could be

no harm in it, he nodded for her to pick it up.

Lassa ran the material of the hat through her fingers. It was of exceptional quality, real black fur felt. The hat itself was now virtually shapeless, having been crushed in numerous

scuffles, and Lassa noticed that the milliner's name had been stitched into the lining: B C

Darling, Milliner, together with the letters JC in a larger, italic stitch just above.

"JC. What do you suppose this means?" Lassa asked the captain, fingering the fine

embroidery.

"Mr Groombridge thought it might be somebody's initials."

"But Mr Menzies' initials are MM, not JC, which could suggest that this wasn't his hat at

all, that it has been placed on his head – " She stopped, conscious that she was beginning to

ramble.

Captain Bywater took the hat from her hands and replaced it back onto the table.

"Stop jumping to conclusions and clutching at straws," he said. "It could also suggest that

Mr Menzies had stolen it from one of his earlier victims, somebody with the initials JC," he

said.

"Yes, I suppose," said Lassa, disheartened.

"Well, good day to you Captain Bywater, sir," Lydia said at her side.

"Yes, once again, thank you for your time, sir," Lassa said.

Once they were clear of the captain's house, Lydia turned to Lassa, saying, "Fat lot of

good that did. We'll never be able to prove my father isn't Dan Dandy. And certainly not in

a week!"

"Don't be so defeatist, Lydia," Lassa chided her gently.

"But it's true! What proof do we have?" she said, more to herself than to Lassa. "None!"

she declared dully. "That's what proof we have! It's not as though we have anything to go

on!"

"On the contrary, Lydia," Lassa said with a smile. "We do have something to go on." She

hooked an arm through Lydia's. "Come on, we have work to do."

"We do?"

"Most definitely," said Lassa coyly. "Now tell me, where can we find Mr Darling, the

milliner?"

Chapter Nine

The Milliner

Mr Darling's neat little millinery shop stood quite remote from all the other places of

business in the village square. Almost concealed behind a row of similar three storey wooden

framed houses, its high door opened into a small alleyway that ran adjacent to the busy street

running towards St Mary Magdalene's church.

The hats in the window soaked up the sunshine and stopped the village pavement traffic,

with their archly angled brims and quivering silk arrows.

When Lassa and Lydia entered into the shop, it was a blaze of candlelight. Hats for every

occasion adorned the shelves, front and back: Straw hats, poke bonnets, headgear beautified

by lace trim, ribbons and feathers. All shapes and designs were represented here.

Lydia had already warned Lassa of Mr Darling's habit of only selling his hats to anyone of pedigree. Many a farmer's wife or cobbler's daughter had been shooed away from his store

empty-handed, simply because they did not fit the criteria of his select clientele. Only the

very aristocratic wore a Darling design.

As a consequence, Lassa did not anticipate her congenial questioning to do down well with

the gentleman, who was now observing them closely from behind the counter.

Mr Darling was a small, respectable-looking man with a sharp eye for business, a man who

had dedicated his life to millinery and to his shop. He had a pinched mouth and small round

eyes that scrutinised every move Lassa and Lydia made.

"Can I help you?" he asked, although his tone suggested that he had no great desire to.

Lassa got straight to the point. "Do you keep a record of your hat sales?"

"Yes of course," Mr Darling snapped. It was obvious that he resented the question.

"Please do not touch the hats," he told Lydia as she went to reach out to a wide-brimmed,

plumed gentlewoman's hat that had caught her fancy. "They are all so very delicate."

"May we look at it?" Lassa persisted.

Mr Darling spluttered with laughter, but the amusement did not reach his cold, unfeeling

eyes.

"Of course not!" he snapped again.

"We have good reason," Lassa said.

"That may very well be," Mr Darling said, staring at her dispassionately, "but nobody is

taking a look inside my sales ledger, not even King George himself." His eyes fluttered

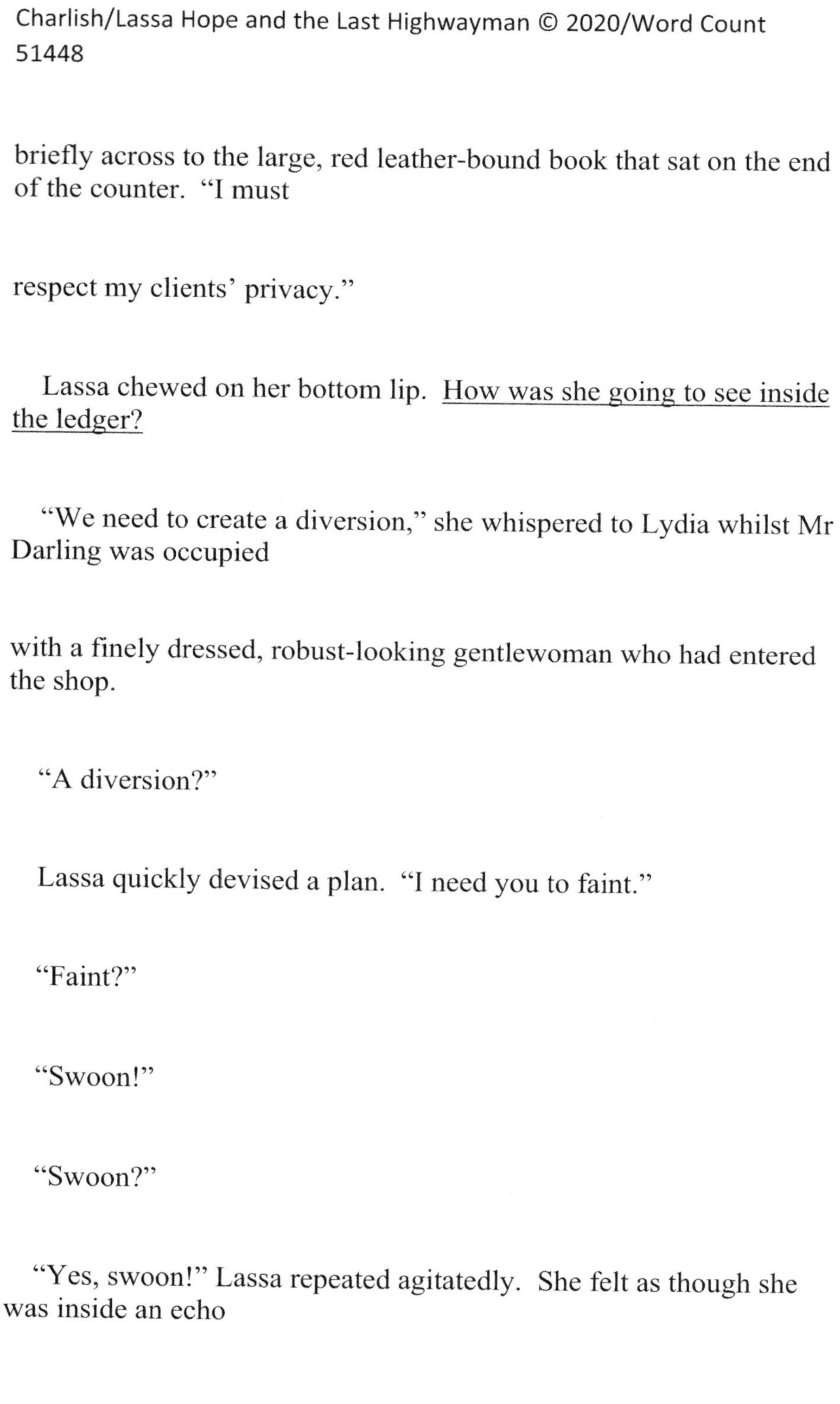

briefly across to the large, red leather-bound book that sat on the end of the counter. “I must

respect my clients’ privacy.”

Lassa chewed on her bottom lip. How was she going to see inside the ledger?

“We need to create a diversion,” she whispered to Lydia whilst Mr Darling was occupied

with a finely dressed, robust-looking gentlewoman who had entered the shop.

“A diversion?”

Lassa quickly devised a plan. “I need you to faint.”

“Faint?”

“Swoon!”

“Swoon?”

“Yes, swoon!” Lassa repeated agitatedly. She felt as though she was inside an echo chamber. "I need you to pretend to pass out. Do you think you can do it?"

"I don't think – no – I don't think I could," Lydia said, shaking her head.

"Not even for your father?"

Lydia sighed, relenting. "Say I do, say I pretend to pass out – " – her eyes darted

nervously from Lassa over to Mr Darling, then back again – " – what will you do?"

"I'll steal the ledger. I'll bet my life that it's that red leather-bound book sitting on the

counter over there."

Lydia looked as though she would pass out for real. The colour drained from her cheeks

and her brow moistened with a nervous perspiration.

"What?" She stared at Lassa, utterly agog. "You can't be serious! You could end up in the stocks. Or worse. You could be transported to a penal colony for theft!"

Lassa gave a nonchalant shrug. She wasn't too sure what a penal colony was. "It's a risk

I'm prepared to take. For your father's sake," she said pointedly.

Lydia was swayed. Lassa was right. At this moment clearing her father's name was the

most important thing in the world. She looked across at Mr Darling. He had lowered a hat

onto the robust lady's head and was now busy picking and preening at its plume. He could

be heard complimenting her on how spectacular it looked and how much younger it made her

appear. Lying evidently came easily to him.

Lydia began a mental countdown from five to one: Five – Four – Three -Two – One. And

on the count of one she raised the back of her hand to her brow and allowed her knees to buckle. Then with a heavy sigh worthy of an Academy Award nomination, she keeled over

onto the shop floor.

Mr Darling and the robust lady exchanged horrified glances, then rushed forward to bend

over her anxiously.

"Gracious!" the robust lady declared, fanning Lydia's face with a lack lustre wave of her

hand. "Do you think she has a fever?"

Whilst Mr Darling was distracted, Lassa hurried over to the counter and grabbed the

ledger. She tucked it under her arm, hiding it within the folds of her cloak, then rushed back

to Lydia, dropping onto her haunches at her side.

"She'll be fine in a minute," she told the milliner and his robust customer bracingly.

"She's always doing this." She pulled Lydia abruptly to her feet. "She just needs some fresh

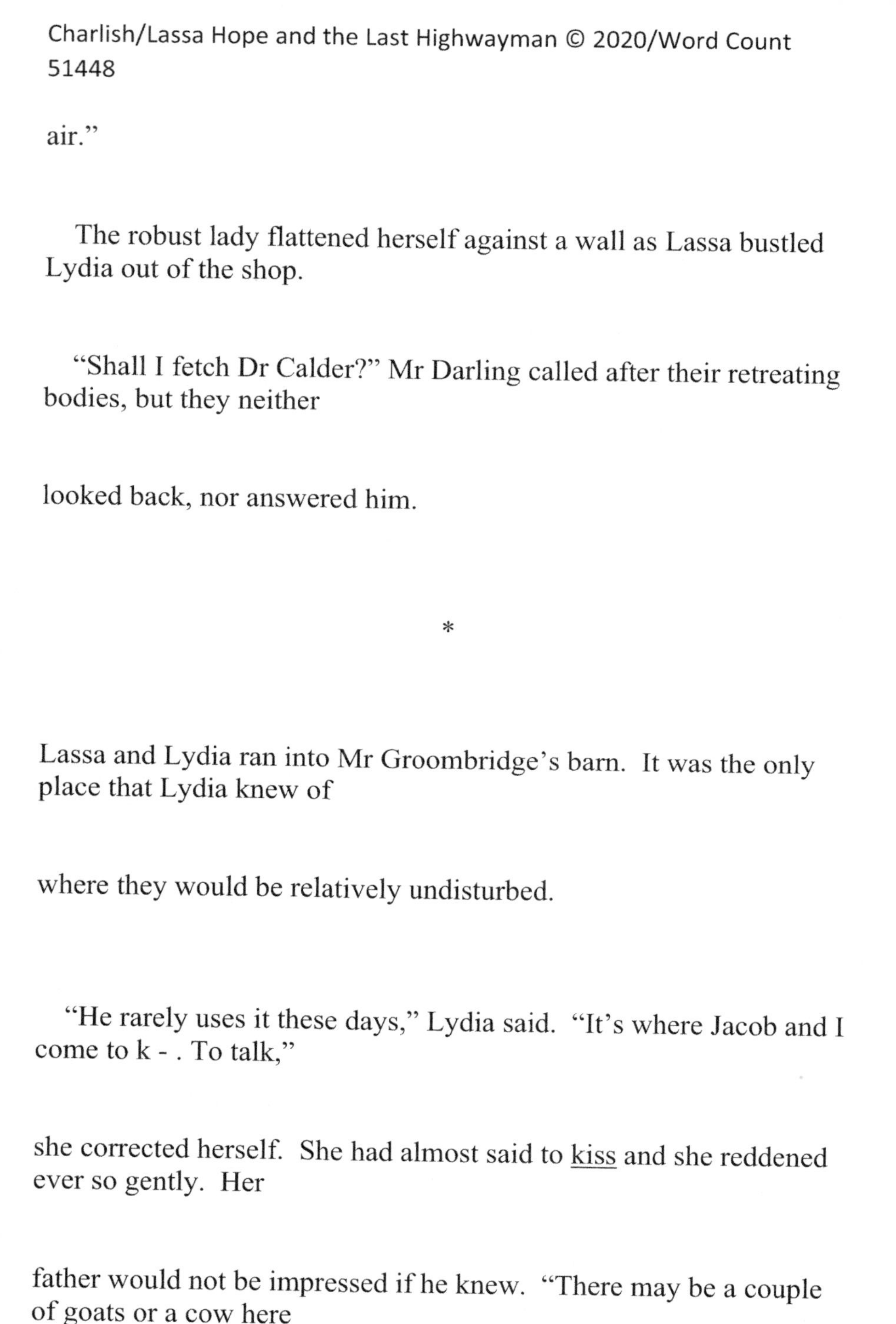

air."

The robust lady flattened herself against a wall as Lassa bustled Lydia out of the shop.

"Shall I fetch Dr Calder?" Mr Darling called after their retreating bodies, but they neither

looked back, nor answered him.

*

Lassa and Lydia ran into Mr Groombridge's barn. It was the only place that Lydia knew of

where they would be relatively undisturbed.

"He rarely uses it these days," Lydia said. "It's where Jacob and I come to k - . To talk,"

she corrected herself. She had almost said to kiss and she reddened ever so gently. Her

father would not be impressed if he knew. "There may be a couple of goats or a cow here some days, but mostly it's empty."

They sat cross-legged on the barn floor and flipped open the red leather-bound book before

them. To Lassa's relief it proved to be the sales ledger she had hoped it would be.

"This will help us a great deal," she said excitedly, drawing her right forefinger down the

neat list of entries.

She lifted her head to see Lydia staring at her in disbelief.

"Can you really read?" Lydia asked incredulously. "Or are you just pretending?"

Lassa thought it churlish to lie. "Yes, I can read very well," she admitted.

"And write too?"

Lassa nodded.

Lydia regarded her in awe and admiration. "You are amazing, Lassa, you really are," she

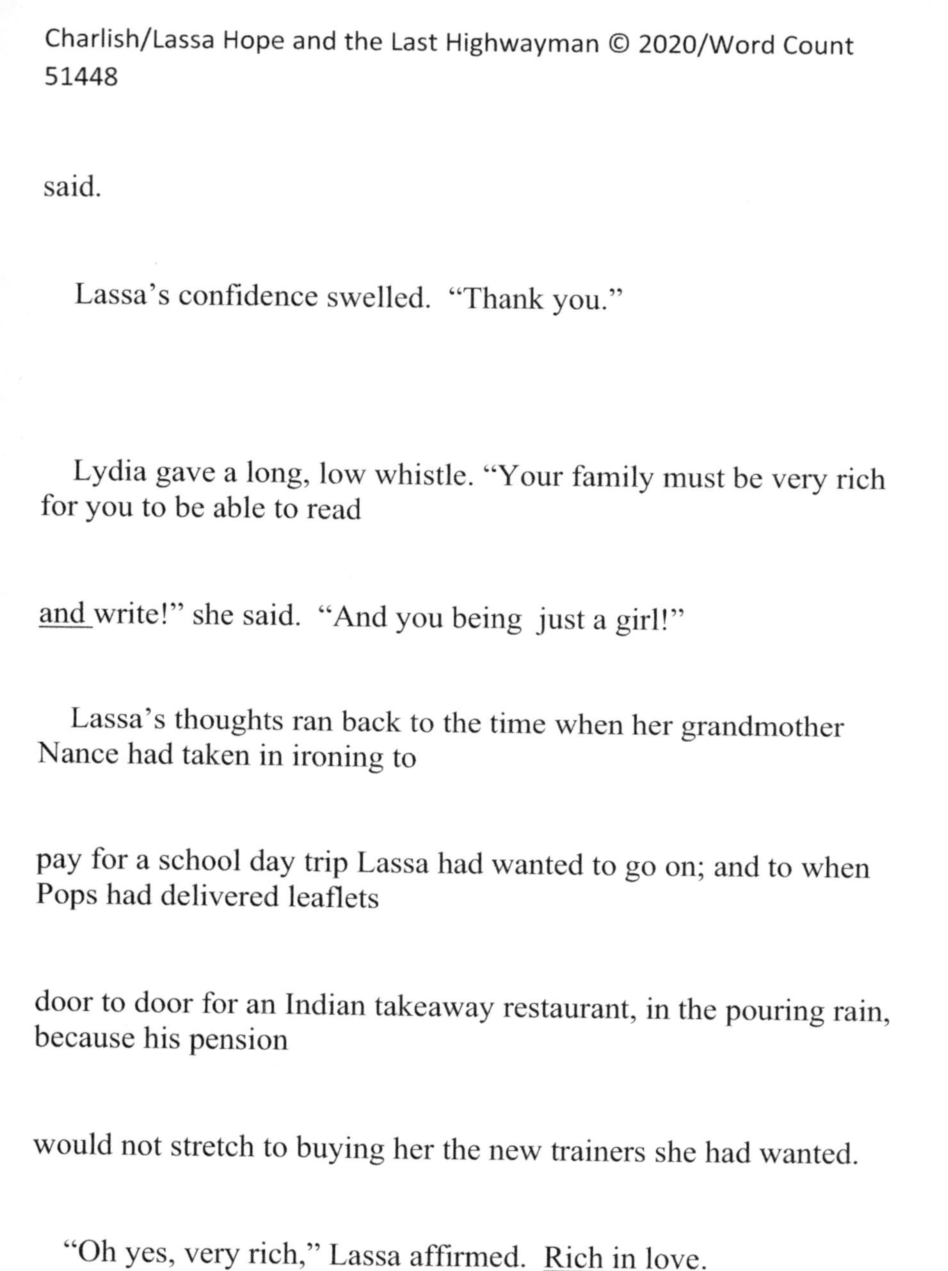

said.

Lassa's confidence swelled. "Thank you."

Lydia gave a long, low whistle. "Your family must be very rich for you to be able to read

and write!" she said. "And you being just a girl!"

Lassa's thoughts ran back to the time when her grandmother Nance had taken in ironing to

pay for a school day trip Lassa had wanted to go on; and to when Pops had delivered leaflets

door to door for an Indian takeaway restaurant, in the pouring rain, because his pension

would not stretch to buying her the new trainers she had wanted.

"Oh yes, very rich," Lassa affirmed. Rich in love.

"It must cost them a small fortune to have you schooled," Lydia looked completely flabbergasted and just a little bit envious. “You are so fortunate!”

Lassa felt very humbled.

“Yes, I am fortunate,” she said, thinking of her home back in the 21st Century and all the

things she had taken for granted: Sanitation, education, transportation, health care and a good,

varied diet that didn’t always have to include parsnips.

She turned back to the ledger.

“This,” she said to Lydia, tapping the book, “is the chief book of accounts for Mr Darling’s

milliner’s shop. It gives a detailed account of all his transactions since – ” - she leafed

backwards through the pages – “ - since March 1762.”

Lydia did not understand.

“So?” she prompted, scratching her head and looking perplexed. Her hair spilled out from under her muslin cap. "How can this book help us to free my father?"

"The tricorn hat that he was found wearing belonged not to him, of course, but to Dan

Dandy." She put her head on one side and regarded Lydia evenly. "The initials JC were

stitched into the rim. So anyone who bought a tricorn hat from Mr Darling – and who also

has the initials JC – is a possible suspect."

"I see," said Lydia, but she did not. Not entirely.

"It's a starting point," Lassa said. She pulled the ledger onto her lap and scanned the

pages. "Look here, since 1762 there have been just six people with the initials JC who have

purchased a three-pointed hat."

Lydia moved closer to look at the ledger over Lassa's shoulder. The mishmash of letters and numbers may well have been Hieroglyphics for all they meant to her.

"Who are they? I may know them."

Lassa read the six entries out loud.

"Dr John Calder, May 1762, Paid in full, one Half Crown

Mr Jolyon Church, September 1763, Paid in full, 7s, 4d

Lord Jonathan Chaney, May 1764, Owing, 5s, 2d

Mr Joseph Cruickshank, August 1764, Owing, one Crown

Judge James Cobb, September 1764, Paid in full, 7s, 2d

Mr Joseph Creed, November 1764, Paid in full, 8s, 1d

"Well, we can rule out Dr Calder," Lydia said. "He was at our cottage for most of the

evening, looking in on your aunt. He even stayed for a bowl of rabbit stew and only left

when Mr Groombridge called for him to attend to a man who had been injured in the robbery.

That's how we learned of my father's arrest." She stopped suddenly and let out a long sigh,

dropping her head to her chest wearily. "It was such terrible news, but Dr Calder is a good

friend. He returned to our cottage as soon as he could, to check on my mother." Again she

sighed and gave herself a long hug. "She's not taking this at all well. I fear she will become

gravely ill with worry."

Lassa slid an arm around Lydia's shoulders and gave her a squeeze.

"Everything will be okay in the end, you'll see," she said with certainty. "And I agree with

you," she said, returning back to the matter in hand. "Since he has a very strong alibi,

Dr Calder can't possibly be Dan Dandy."

"Alibub?"

"Alibi," Lassa corrected. She thought for a moment, then explained. "Having an alibi

means that somebody other than yourself can testify to the fact that you were somewhere else

at the time a crime was committed."

Lydia nodded ardently in full understanding.

"Then Mr Church and Lord Chaney have an ali-alibi too," she said falteringly.

"How so?"

"They're both dead."

"Oh."

"Then that only leaves Mr Cruickshank, Judge Cobb and Mr Creed," Lydia said matter-of-

factly. "Do we need to check their alibis now?"

"Yes, Lydia, we must. And by a process of elimination, we will find the real Dan

Dandy!" Lassa thumped the ledger shut. "But first we must do something very important."

"What's that?"

"We must return this book to Mr Darling."

Lydia pulled a face.

"We can't keep it forever," Lassa reasoned. "I only ever intended for us to borrow it, not

to steal it."

"I know, I know," Lydia conceded reluctantly. "But this time, if there's any swooning to

be done, you can do it!"

They left Mr Groombridge's farm, hope glimmering brightly in their hearts for the first

time since waking up that morning.

Chapter Ten

A Sudden Realisation

Returning the sales ledger to Mr Darling's millinery shop was no mean feat, but Lassa and

Lydia managed it.

Mr Darling hadn't even noticed it missing, which was a blessing. Lassa knew from her

History lessons at school that it was common for thieves to have their hands chopped off at

the wrists. Or was that Medieval England? Either way, Lassa liked her hands exactly where

they were, thank you very much, and was therefore grateful not to have been caught

red-handed.

Once the ledger was back in its rightful place, Lassa and Lydia set off to their first port of

call, Mr Creed's little house on the hill.

On route, they walked through a field, a field that Lassa recognised at once. The positions

of the trees and many of the shrubs were familiar to her. It was the field into which she had first arrived just a few days ago. She viewed with relief the twigs and bracken that she and

Philomena had fashioned into the shape of a cross to mark the position of the portal, and

in the air just above, the portal's shimmering radiance was still clearly visible to her.

They walked on through the field, past the portal, and as they reached the top of the incline

close to the little house on the hill where Mr Creed resided, a grim outline of a gibbet – a

hangman's tower – came into view, an eerie sight in the distance, at the very edge of a wild

moorland road.

Upon seeing its grisly frame for the first time, Lydia sunk to her knees on the ground and

sobbed as though her heart would break in two.

"I know what you're thinking," Lassa said, almost in tears herself. "But it won't happen.

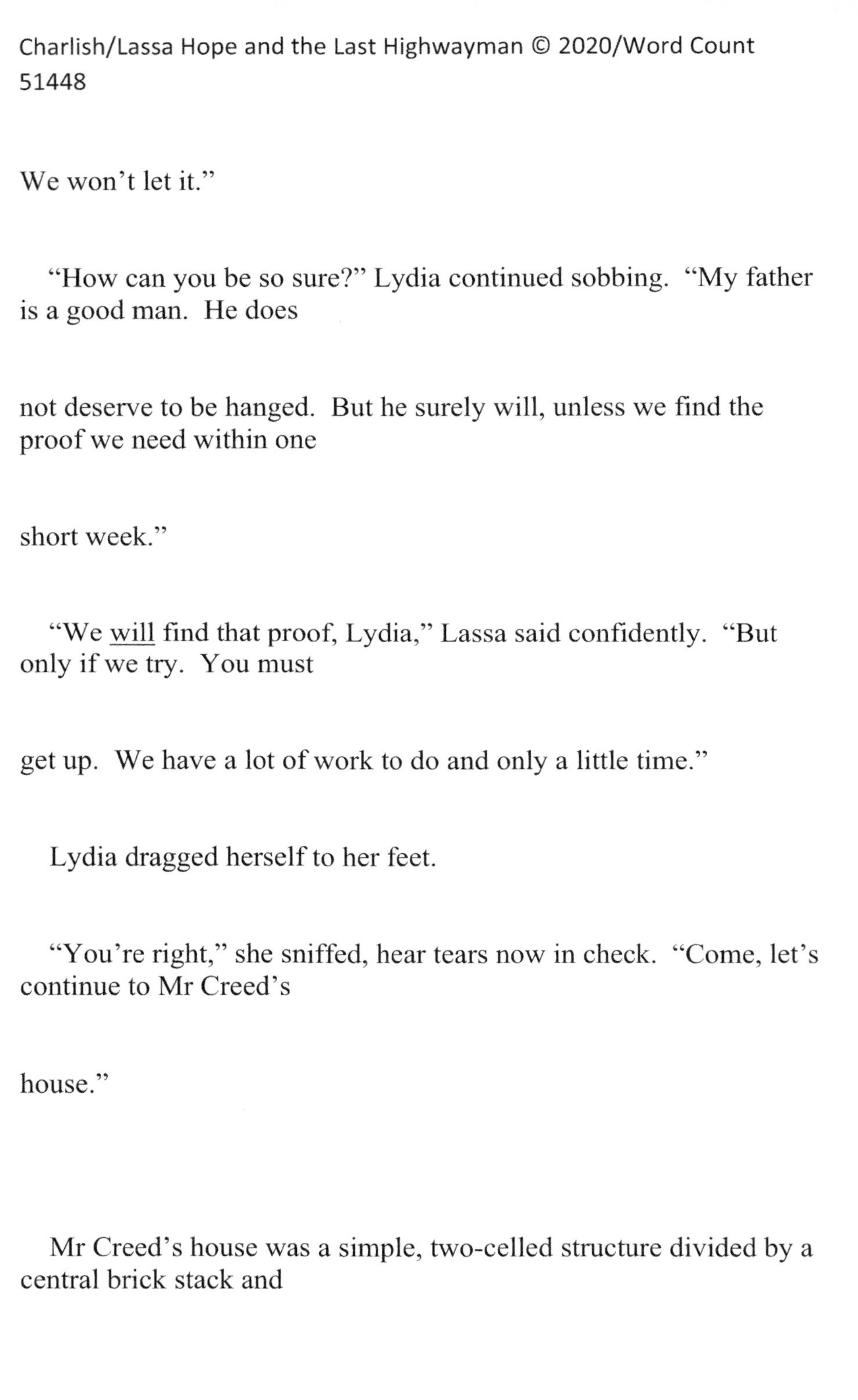

We won't let it."

"How can you be so sure?" Lydia continued sobbing. "My father is a good man. He does not deserve to be hanged. But he surely will, unless we find the proof we need within one short week."

"We will find that proof, Lydia," Lassa said confidently. "But only if we try. You must get up. We have a lot of work to do and only a little time."

Lydia dragged herself to her feet.

"You're right," she sniffed, hear tears now in check. "Come, let's continue to Mr Creed's house."

Mr Creed's house was a simple, two-celled structure divided by a central brick stack and was roofed in thatched sedge. It was dilapidated and the garden was unkempt. It certainly did

not belong to the sort of person Lassa thought might meet the strict criteria of Mr Darling's

elite clientele.

"This can't be right," Lassa muttered.

"Oh but it is," Lydia assured her. "I came here once with my father, to deliver a

weathervane Mr Creed had wanted him to make."

"Your father makes weathervanes?"

"Oh yes. And sundials. And gates. He doesn't just shoe horses. He's very clever."

"But the house looks as though it's deserted," Lassa said. "Is it possible he could have

moved?"

"Moved?"

It was a concept that was completely alien to Lydia. People in 18th Century England did

not move house as frequently as they would three centuries later. Indeed, many people died

without having travelled more than five miles from the houses in which they were born.

A couple walked past the house arm in arm along the pavement and a man with a dog bade

the couple good morning. Two horse-drawn carriages passed one another in the road.

"Never mind," said Lassa. Then, changing the subject, "well, we're not going to find out

anything by standing all day."

She walked boldly up to the door of the house and knocked. Just as she had expected,

nobody answered her call.

"Nobody's home," a young man called to her from the pavement. He was pushing a barrow of vegetables to market. "Mr Creed has gone to stay with his daughter in the Wye

Valley."

"When did he leave?"

"Four or five months ago," the young man replied amiably. "He became a grandfather and

wanted to visit the baby. A boy, I think. Left in a carriage first thing one morning before

Christmas. I gave him an apple for the journey."

And so Lassa and Lydia struck Mr Joseph Creed off their suspect list with a virtual black

marker, and set off to see Judge James Cobb.

*

Judge James Cobb lived at Rycourt Manor with his wife, Mrs Esther Cobb, and their pug,

Murphy.

Lydia had never met him, but she had heard of him. He was more popularly known as Cobb the Cold because of the punishments he meted out. He was fiercely authoritarian in handing out the law, and had even once sentenced a sixteen year old boy to hang for the theft of a twenty five shilling coat.

Few of the villagers had actually seen him either, since he spent most of his time working in London, but still he was notorious for being a thoroughly unpleasant and vile-mannered man. His wife was equally as loathsome, and unlike her husband, was a familiar face in the village, where she was often seen throwing her not inconsiderable weight around, barking orders to her servants.

Lassa knew that a consult with either one of the Cobbs would be far from easy.

At the gates of Rycourt Manor, Lassa and Lydia came across a young man. He had scruffy

brown hair and big doe eyes and he wore a black hat, a brown waist coat and filthy grey

breeches. He carried a pheasant over his shoulder, and a beautiful black Labrador Retriever

stood faithfully at his heel. He seemed familiar to Lassa somehow, but she couldn't quitw

place him.

"Hello Tom," Lydia greeted him.

Tom said nothing, but stared straight ahead.

"Tom?"

"Miss Lydia." Tom broke his silence, but still his eyes did not meet hers, and the tone of

his voice was icy cool.

Lydia dropped her chin to her chest in shame, her cheeks colouring blood red. Suddenly

she knew why he was acting so distant.

"It's not true, you know," she said in a low voice. "My father isn't Dan Dandy. They have

the wrong man, you'll see."

Still Tom refused to look at her. Instead his eyes rested on the brick piers supporting the

manor's imposing, wrought iron double-arched gates.

"Is that so?" He said, apparently unmoved by her words. "Dan Dandy's a wrong 'un. He

almost killed a man. Almost died of fright, he did. Heart nearly stopped beating in his chest

he was so afraid."

Bitter tears stung the back of Lydia's eyes, but she wouldn't give Tom the satisfaction of

seeing them.

Recognising that she was too upset to talk, Lassa spoke for her. "I'm Lassa Hope, a friend

of Mr and Mrs Menzies."

Tom screwed up his big, dark eyes.

"Then I suggest you find better friends, Miss Hope," he said malevolently. "The friends of

highwaymen aren't welcome in this village."

"My father is not a highwayman!" Lydia protested, unable to contain herself. She

trembled with still-hidden tears. The ball of hope that had glimmered in her heart earlier had

now sunk like a pebble in a pond. "He is not, I tell you!"

Tom gave a snort of incredulity.

"Rubbish! I saw it all. I saw him, your father, Dan Dandy." His eyes mocked her. "I was there that night, you see. Your father was dressed in a leather eye mask and a dark

neckerchief and he was holding a pistol. So how do you explain that, eh?"

Lydia took a step forward towards Tom.

"What you saw was a lie!" she hissed. "Had you arrived at the scene just moments earlier

you would have seen the truth!"

Tom raised a brow in curiosity. "Which is?"

Lassa took up the story, suddenly placing Tom as one of the villagers who turned up at the

scene that night. He had been carrying a burning torch and the flame had lit up his face.

"That the real Dan Dandy knocked Mr Menzies to the floor, unconscious, dressed him in his

highwayman's disguise and then fled, like the coward he is, leaving Mr Menzies to face the charges to a crime which he did not commit."

Tom hooted with laughter and his whole body shook. The vibrations freed feathers from

the pheasant hanging down his back and they flew gently into the air around him.

"Do you expect me to believe that?" he said harshly.

Lassa did not reply, instead contenting herself by glaring angrily at him. He glared right

back.

"It's true!" Lydia spat the words. "Lassa was there, hidden in a ditch by the road. She saw

it all."

Tom shrugged his shoulders, as though the truth did not matter to him anyway.

"Do you remember what Mr Menzies said when you pulled him to his feet?" Lassa asked

him rhetorically. "He said, 'You've got it all wrong'." She paused momentarily to take a breath, hoping to shock him with her words. It worked. Tom's eyes clouded over with a

faraway look and his face became pinched as he tried to recollect the night's events.

"I can tell you everything," Lassa went on. "From the eagle crest on the side of the carriage,

to the colour of the breeches the coachman was wearing. I was there, I tell you. And I saw it

all."

For the next few moments nobody spoke. It was Tom who broke the silence first.

"You were there!" he said at last in a voice so low that it was almost inaudible. His

shocked eyes were as wide as saucers. "Then they will surely hang an innocent man!"

"Not if we can help it," Lassa said, relieved to have finally got Tom on side.

Tom creased his brow. "But how do you know you can prevent it?"

His tone was neither mocking nor scathing, but Lydia was immediately rankled.

"That's none of your concern!" she snapped, still clearly wounded by his earlier words.

The dog at Tom's heel gave a low growl. At first Lydia cowered, but it wasn't Lydia that

had caused the dog's change in behaviour. She was staring intently past Lydia and Lassa,

into a clearing between some birches. Her ears were laid back almost flat, her hackles raised,

her every muscle tensed.

Tom crouched to scratch her ears. "What is it Tilly, old girl?"

The snarling dog continued to stare into the clearing. Lassa and Lydia turned to follow her

line of vision. Leaves crunched. Twigs crackled.

"Someone's coming," Lassa said.

Bit it proved not to be someone, but <u>something</u>.

A short, brown velvet-coated dog appeared, trotting out of the brambly undergrowth, his

head held proud. It looked decidedly square and cobby, and it was snuffling like a small pig.

Tom drew in his breath sharply.

"It's Murphy," he said in a low voice. He patted his dog's back and rose to his feet.

"Judge Cobb and his wife won't be far behind, so if you don't mind, I think I'll take my leave

of you now, before they reach us." He glanced sheepishly behind him, at the pheasant slung

over his shoulder, adding, "Tilly acquired this on their land. I tried to stop her, honest I did,

but it all happened so fast."

Lydia flashed Tom a meaningful look.

"I believe you, Tom," she said, her eyes holding his as he tried to avoid her gaze. "After all, I've known you and your family for years, so when you say you haven't done anything

wrong, I'm always going to accept your word as the truth."

The meaning of her words were not lost on Tom. He swallowed hard and his shoulders

were seen to slump visibly. To his credit, he apologised.

"I'm sorry, Miss Menzies," he said, shame-faced, his brown eyes pleading for

understanding, "Really I am."

Lydia inclined her head in silent forgiveness and Tom thanked her before sloping off with

his loyal black Labrador Retriever in tow.

Lassa and Lydia looked towards the clearing, awaiting Judge Cobb's appearance into it,

their hearts quickening.

But when he did finally appear, just moments later, their jaws dropped in surprise.

Judge Cobb was barely five foot in height and as round as he was tall. He had a red,

bloated head and blunt features, and as he drew nearer Lassa and Lydia noticed that he

walked with a definite gait to his left side.

That they had ever suspected this man of being Dan Dandy was patently laughable. Not

only was he too small and too round, the man could scarcely carry himself five feet without

having to stop to catch his breath.

"Gerrouta here," he yelled, bumbling nearer and nearer, huffing and puffing, and shaking

the cane that he used for support high in the air. His moon face was red with anger.

"Gerraway from my gate, I say!"

Lassa and Lydia apologised immediately and ran off.

There was just one more person on their suspect list.

Mr Joseph Cruickshank.

*

By the time they reached Urton Hall, both Lassa and Lydia were hungry, cold and exhausted.

It had been a very long day. But it wasn't over yet. They still needed to discover whether or

not Joseph Cruickshank had an alibi for the night Moses was apprehended. And if he did –

and it checked out – then they were back to square one.

A lot was riding on this visit to Urton Hall. And they both knew it. They met Joseph

Cruickshank exercising a young mare in a field beside the stable yard. The mare was moving

in a large circle in a half trot/ half parade motion, and was tethered by two reins, both of

which Cruickshank had a hold.

It was a full ten minutes before he spotted Lassa and Lydia, who were watching the display

from a discreet distance. He turned away with a contemptuous smile.

"If you're after the money I owe Menzies then you're out of luck," he called to them

without averting his eyes from his mare. He allowed his reign to dangle a little as he brought

her to a canter. "He discharged the debt and besides, a highwayman has no creditors."

Lassa took three bold steps forward.

"We haven't come for the money," she told him, moving resolutely forward.

"Oh?" he said.

"We've come to talk about the hat he was wearing when he was apprehended."

A flicker of irritation crossed Cruickshank's face. He brought the mare to a halt and called for Isaac, who emerged running from stables.

"Take her to graze with the others," he barked, handing Isaac the reins.

Isaac glanced briefly Lassa and Lydia's way, then trudged off in the direction of the next

field, where White Lightning and a few other horses could already be seen grazing on the

green pasture.

Cruickshank brushed his palms together to dispel the grease from the reins, and stepped

forward. He was now standing so close to Lassa that she could feel his breath on her face.

She shrank away, partly through intimidation, but mostly due to his fetid breath, which was

foul with the stench of ale and tobacco.

"I'm a very busy man, girl," he said. "What has Menzies' hat got to do with me?"

"They – they say it could possibly have belonged to you," Lassa informed him. She

paused for a moment, waiting for his reaction. She didn't think a little white lie could do any

harm. In fact, she thought it might be able to help. "They say it has your initials sewn into it.

JC," she continued. Behind her back her fingers were crossed. "They wonder how

Mr Menzies could have acquired your hat unless he is telling the truth when he says that he

blacked out after being struck by the real Dan Dandy, only to regain consciousness a little

while later, wearing his disguise. They say that the real Dan Dandy could have dressed

Mr Menzies like that, while he was out cold, to incriminate him."

Lassa did not believe there was enough space between them for Cruickshank to make

another prowling step towards her, but he managed it nonetheless.

His lips thinned and his eyes narrowed. "They?" he said sinisterly. "Who are 'They'?"

Lassa backed away, wary now. She licked her lips nervously.

"I've said too much," she said, feigning innocence. "No doubt they will want to speak to

you themselves sooner or later."

"Oh will they indeed?" Cruickshank's voice practically dripped sarcasm, then,

menacingly, "well, they will be given the same answer that I am going to give you." His eyes

glittered with anger. "I. Have. No. Idea," he punctuated each word stiffly for effect.

There was an ominous silence. Neither Lassa nor Lydia, nor Cruickshank moved. It was as

though the earth had stopped spinning.

A small gasp escaping Cruickshank's thin lips broke the silence. "Ah, I rem -" - he cut off mid-syllable, his brow wrinkled in thought - " – yes, indeed, I remember now. I was held up

by Dan Dandy – Moses Menzies – " - he added pointedly for Lydia's benefit – " – sometime

last year. The scoundrel stole my hat, among other things." He stared at Lassa head

on. "That must be how he came to possess my hat. If, indeed, it is my hat at all."

Lassa's heart skipped a beat. She had completely forgotten Dr Calder saying that

Cruickshank himself had been held up by the highwayman. With hope giving way to

despondency, it suddenly occurred to her that Cruickshank could be telling the truth! And if

that was the case, if his hat had been stolen as he claimed, then Dan Dandy could be any man

in England.

She looked across at Lydia and noticed the tears forming in the corners of her eyes.

Evidently, the same thought had occurred to her too.

Lassa sighed heavily and spoke very quietly, her eyes downcast.

"We'll take our leave of you, sir," she said. She felt so disheartened and upset that the

words nearly caught in her throat. "We are sorry to have troubled you."

Cruickshank's lips curled into a smirk. "It's no bother," he said, then turned on his heels to

join Isaac and the horses in the next field.

Lassa and Lydia plodded off, their hearts heavy. They said nothing, but thoughts of the

incarcerated Moses filled their minds. The cold wind whipped at their hair and clothes, but

they were in no rush to get home.

They stopped off at the stream, sitting contemplatively at its edge for an hour or more, tossing shiny tan pebbles and watching in silence as they bounced off the water's surface.

Deep in thought, Lassa picked up a handful of earth and sifted it through her fingers,

allowing it to fall into a pile at her side.

"Perhaps history can't be changed after all," she thought to herself miserably. "I have

failed this family."

And yet she was still convinced that she had travelled through time for a reason, that the

creation of the wormhole was no accident. That there had to be a purpose to her being here.

"Have you ever been to a public hanging?" Lydia asked Lassa out of the blue.

Lassa shuddered at the very thought of it and shook her head. She had seen many artists'

impressions, but of course she had never actually been a witness to one.

"No," she said.

Lydia stopped throwing pebbles into the stream and hugged her knees to her chest. She

stared straight ahead, her eyes dull and unseeing.

"Nor I," she muttered miserably. "But I've heard what happens."

In spite of herself Lassa found herself listening to Lydia as she told her of a recent multiple

hanging at Tyburn, where a dozen criminals had been hanged at the same time.

"They were hanged from two parallel beams, then the platform was released by moving a

pin that acted as a drawbar under the drop." Lydia shivered involuntarily. "Death by

hanging is rarely instantaneous, so I hear. A horrible and cruel death it is."

Lassa took a hold of Lydia's hand. Lydia continued to stare straight ahead.

"Of course they will want to make an example of my father, so he will be hanged alone,"

Lydia went on matter-of-factly. "He will be hooded, then led from the Condemned Hold into

the Press Yard, where his leg irons will be removed and his hands tied. Then he will be led

out through the Debtor's Door and up a short flight of stairs onto the gallows, where he

will be noosed, then hanged by the neck until dead."

So great was her grief that she burst into uncontrollable tears.

"The crowds will be delighted," she continued, trembling violently. "They will cheer and

whoop with joy, glad in the knowledge that justice has finally been served. That Dan Dandy

is dead." She turned to Lassa with despair in her eyes. "But it won't be over, even then. His

lifeless body will be brought back here in a four wheeled wagon, gibbeted, exposed to the public as a constant reminder of his guilt, and as a deterrent to those considering a similar life

of crime."

Two small hot tears broke away from Lassa's eyes and stole down her freckled cheeks.

"It won't happen," she said, The stern resolve she had made to prove Moses' innocence

had returned. "We'll – "

Lydia sprang to her feet.

"We'll what?" she screamed, her face blotchy and stained with tears. "It's hopeless, can't

you see that? Oh, I should never have listened to you. You're just a silly little girl!"

She raised her petticoats and ran off, leaving Lassa alone at the side of the stream, her eyes

blinded with tears.

Lassa couldn't blame Lydia for feeling the way she did. Ever since Moses had been arrested, Lassa had been promising to unearth the proof that would secure his release. And

with no proof forthcoming, it was of little wonder that Lydia was angry with her, and

resented her for having given her false hope.

Lassa could have kicked herself for being so stupidly arrogant. It had to be avoided as

much as the timidness that she had hid behind in the 21st Century.

She remained alone with her thoughts by the steam until it grew dark. Then she made a

slow walk back to the Menzies' cottage.

She entered into the cottage soundlessly to find Mary seated in the chair by the fire. The

twins were asleep on her lap, their mouths wide open, breathing loudly. She looked

exhausted and wretched in misery. When she saw Lassa she smiled sadly.

"Lydia came in a while ago," she said in a voice low so as not to wake either of the twins.

"She told me what you have been doing all day, and what happened. Thank you for trying."

Lassa knelt on the floor at Mary's feet.

"I'm so sorry," she whispered. "I really thought I would be able to help."

"I know," said Mary with a heavy heart. She shifted to get more comfortable under the

twins' weight and accidently woke Temperance, who immediately asked for her father.

"Your father has gone away for a little while," Mary told her softly, stroking her face.

Temperance closed her eyes and drifted off to sleep again.

"Go to bed, Lassa," Mary said. "You've had a long day."

A lump rose in Lassa's throat. The pain and anguish this family was going through just wasn't fair. Moses was an innocent man.

She left the room as silently as she had entered it and made her way upstairs towards

Philomena's room. She pushed the door ajar, but on seeing the regular rise and fall of the

blankets, she realised that the Professor was sound asleep, and so she decided not to disturb

her, despite desperately needing to talk to her.

Lying in her own bed in Esme's room, Lassa ran over the course of events in her mind. It

had started out so well, with Captain Bywater agreeing to meet with her and Lydia, even

allowing them to hold Dan Dandy's hat.

And then, suddenly, she remembered the captain's response when she had queried why

Moses Menzies would own a hat with the initials JC stitched into it.

"It could….suggest that he had stolen it from one of his earlier victims, somebody with the initials JC."

The captain's words rang as clear as a bell in her head. Oh, why hadn't she listened to

him? Then she might have considered other avenues of investigation, rather than pinning all

her hopes on this one, and spending an entire day barking up the wrong tree.

It was, of course, quite reasonable to assume that Joseph Cruickshank was telling the truth.

He had fallen victim to Dan Dandy himself in June of 1764 – Dr Calder had confirmed it –

and so it was quite possible that his hat had been stolen by Dan Dandy and then worn by him

in all subsequent robberies.

Lassa conceded to that the fact that although Joseph Cruickshank did not honour his debts,

and despite the fact that he was not the most likeable of men, it did not make him a highwayman.

Lassa lay her head back on her pillow and closed her eyes.

KAZAM!

Lassa was jolted from her dreamless sleep by a single thought that caused her to sit bolt

upright in bed, her heart beating like a kettle drum.

"Of course!" she cried out into the darkness of the room.

Within seconds Esme was awake, rubbing at her eyes and Mary and Lydia were at her

door, holding candles that threw light into the gloom.

"Lassa?" Mary said, her eyes flickering with concern in the glimmering light. "Did you

have a nightmare?"

"Joseph Cruickshank couldn't possibly had had his hat stolen when he was held up by Dan

Dandy!" Lassa blurted.

Mary and Lydia sat themselves down on the end of her bed. Esme moved into the

candlelight.

"It's true!" Lassa continued breathlessly. "He was held up by Dan Dandy in June of last

year, but he didn't buy the hat from Mr Darling's shop until the following August."

"So - ?"

"So how could his hat have been stolen, when he hadn't even purchased it yet?"

Mary, Lydia and Esme observed Lassa with renewed hope daring to creep into their

hearts.

"Do you think that Mr Cruickshank is Dan Dandy, Lassa?" asked Mary, her voice thick with emotion.

“Yes, I do,” Lassa said. “And I have thought of other ways to prove it.” She looked at

Lydia, whose face was so pale it seemed to shine with a light of its own. “Will you help me

tomorrow? I believe I can clear your father’s name.”

Lydia drew in a ragged breath and flung her arms around Lassa’s neck, crying with

emotion.

“I’m sorry,” she sobbed tears of joy. “I should never have yelled at you.”

“Shhhh…” Lassa hugged Lydia back. “Everything is going to be just fine.”

Chapter Eleven

Lassa's Plan

Breakfast the next morning was a far more lavish affair than was usual. Dr Calder's

housemaid called round with a ham, and Mary boiled it and served it up with eggs and

tomatoes from the garden.

Everybody seemed in a chirpier, less pessimistic frame of mind. Once more there was

noisy chatter at the dining table, and not of Moses' incarceration at Newgate Prison, or of the

possibility of him dying of typhus – the so-called jail-fever – before ever reaching the

gallows. Instead there was talk of the future and of their hopes and plans as a family.

Philomena proved well enough to breakfast in the dining room for the first time since

being brought to the Menzies' cottage. Her aches and pains had diminished greatly and her bruises, although still discolouring her face and hands, appeared to be healing nicely.

Like Lassa, she too was anxious to leave the 18th Century as soon as possible. She was

keen to go home, back to her own normality of marking homework and invigilating

examinations. But having spoken to Lassa, and having heard all about Joseph Cruickshank

and the evidence surrounding the tricorn hat, she was more than happy to stay a little

while longer, until Moses had been spared the hangman's noose.

"I have no idea what we'll say when we get home," Philomena said in a low voice as Mary

and Lydia began to clear the breakfast things away.

Esme and the twins rushed past her in their haste to get outside in the garden to play. They

knocked at her chair, making her wince as her already bruised ribs were pushed into the table.

"We've been gone for days," she continued. "Your parents will think I've kidnapped

you."

"Grandparents," Lassa corrected her quietly. "My parents were killed when I was a baby,

in a road accident."

"Oh I'm sorry to hear that," Philomena said. She hadn't known.

"But, you're right," Lassa's voice sounded shaky. "We will have to think of something to

explain where we have been, and why we have been so long."

Philomena laughed, but the humour did not reach her eyes. "It will have to be something

good!"

Lassa lapsed into thoughtful silence, while Philomena finished off the last of her warm

milk.

Lydia re-entered the room.

"What must we do next to prove that Joseph Cruickshank is the real Dan Dandy?" she

asked, drawing up a chair next to Lassa's. It was evident that she was eager to clear her

father's name, and to see him freed as soon as possible.

"We must return to the location of the last highway robbery, where your father was

apprehended," Lassa said.

Lydia and Philomena looked at each other, bewildered.

"I need to check the ground there," Lassa told them, deliberately not giving too much

away. "If what I expect to find is evident, then we'll have all the proof we need to convince

Captain Bywater of Mr Menzies' innocence."

"And of Mr Cruickshank's guilt?" Philomena asked.

Lassa nodded. "Absolutely," she said.

Lydia's mouth broadened into a happy smile.

"Then what are we waiting for?" she said, rising to her feet. "We must go to this place at

once." She swept out of the room, calling over her shoulder, "I'll fetch out shawls."

"I hope you know what you're doing, Lassa," Philomena said once she was certain Lydia

had moved out of earshot. Her words were calmly spoken, but there was a troubled look

about her eyes. "There are going to be so many disappointed people if you fail to find what

you're looking for. And one hanged man," she added meaningfully.

Lassa rose from her seat slowly and gave Philomena a fleeting smile. "I know, but I'm

confident I'll be able to pull it off."

Philomena looked up at her from under her fringe of grey hair, her darks eyes penetrating.

"The justice system here is not what it is a home, Lassa," she reminded her soberly.

"Moses won't be afforded the fair trial that he would have received had he lived in the 21st

Century." She sighed, her gaze not wavering from Lassa's face for a second. "In the 1700s

trials were very short, some not lasting more than half an hour. And the jurors

didn't just hear the one trial, but half a dozen or so, before retiring to consider their verdicts.

Often they didn't even retire to debate the case; they just huddled in a corner and had quick

chat."

"I believe I will prove Mr Menzies' innocence before he goes to trial," Lassa smiled, with

an unreadable expression beneath the surface.

"But how?" Philomena reasoned. "What real proof will you have? There's no DNA

testing, no fingerprint analysis, no firearm examinations, no CCTV. I could go on."

Philomena sighed heavily and shook her head. "There's no presumption of innocence and no

right to remain silent. In the time we find ourselves living in now, defendants are expected to

disprove the evidence presented against them and establish their innocence. The opinion was

that if the defendants were innocent, they ought to be able to prove it, And you have <u>one</u>

piece of evidence, just one, Lassa. And even that is hardly conclusive."

"For the moment," Lassa said stiltedly.

"For the moment," Philomena echoed. "Which is flimsy at best," she reminded. "But in

the 18th Century witness testimony was the most common source of evidence, and in this case there are at least a dozen, highly respected men of the village who will testify that they

apprehended Moses Menzies dressed as a highwayman and – the most damning part of

it all – that he was in possession of a firearm."

Lassa pushed aside the thought that Philomena could be right. At the moment her vision

was tunnelled towards one thing and one thing only, to find the evidence she needed to prove

Mr Menzies' innocence.

Lassa's gaze strayed to the door as a be-shawled Lydia rushed back into the room. She

crouched down so that her mouth was level with Philomena's ear.

"I know what you're saying," Lassa said in a whisper. "But it will be okay. Trust me."

Philomena threw back her hands in surrender. "Okay, okay." Her face relaxed into a smile. "Then there's nothing left for me to say except good luck." Her words were heartfelt.

"And be careful."

With a brief nod of her head, Lassa got to her feet and headed out of the door, biting back

the urge to remind Philomena that being careful didn't come into it. She needed to save

Moses Menzies' life. At all costs.

*

Lassa was able to identify the exact spot in the road where Dan Dandy held up his last

carriage by the many footprints, paw prints, hoof prints and wheel tracks that were still

clearly visible in the ground there. The rain had not fallen since that fateful night, and the mud had since dried to leave perfectly intact imprints imbedded in the soil.

Lassa lowered herself onto her haunches by the trench where she and Moses had secreted

themselves, and studied the ground there. Lydia watched over her, bewildered but silent,

drawing her shawl tightly around her body as a cool breeze picked up.

For a while Lassa retreated into herself, completely immersed in her own thoughts as she

meticulously and methodically studied the patterns on the floor, wanting to leave nothing to

chance. She dropped her hand to a hoof print and allowed a small, satisfied smile to curl her

lips as her fingers carefully traced its outline. It was exactly what she had hoped to find. She

reproached herself for any earlier doubts that she had had, and sprang immediately to her

feet. She could not hope to conceal her delight. She regarded Lydia with a face which was as elated as her own.

"Joseph Cruickshank was here that night, Lydia," she confirmed excitedly. "I know that

now without a shadow of a doubt." She licked her suddenly dry lips, "And he wasn't among

the men from the village because I don't recollect seeing him. Besides, they all arrived on

foot and this – " - she pointed to the hoof print at her feet – " – this proves that Cruickshank

was on horseback. And since there was only the one person on horseback that evening, and

since that person was the highwayman, it can only mean one thing." Her eyes lit up. When

she next spoke, it was slowly, so that their full meaning would not be lost on Lydia.

"Cruickshank is the highwayman. He is Dan Dandy."

"You say you can prove it?" Lydia asked with more than a hint of admiration. "Is it the conclusive evidence that Captain Bywater said we needed to find?"

"Most definitely," Lassa glanced up. Slate grey clouds, thick like cotton wool, were

scudding across the sky. "Provided, of course, that the rain holds off." She sighed. Though

the clouds were dark and there was no precipitation in the air, it did not bode well. "We must

act fast. If it rains, these prints – and our proof along with them – will be washed away

forever."

Lydia nodded. She did not realise the significance of the prints on the ground, but she

knew they were important to Lassa, and so she found herself silently praying that the heavens

would not open.

"What must we do now?" She tried to speak in her natural tone, but only a whisper escaped her dry lips. All of a sudden her body was hit with a nervous excitement.

Lassa did not reply. She was deep in thought again, scratching her chin and staring up into

the dull sky.

"Lassa?" Lydia promoted, fixing her trusting hazel eyes upon her face. She absently

chewed on her bottom lip, trying to guess what Lassa's next move would be. "Lassa, what

must we do now?"

Lassa was awoken from her thoughts.

"We must speak with Joseph Cruickshank's stable boy, Isaac," she said. "We're going to

need his help."

They grimaced at each other in unison. They both knew that soliciting Isaac's help wouldn't be easy. For Isaac to assist Lassa and Lydia in obtaining incriminating evidence

against his master would be extremely dangerous, and for him to agree to doing it in the first

place would be nothing short of a miracle. Lassa wished there was another way, but she

didn't know of one.

They tramped across the fields towards Urton Hall, willing the cumulus clouds above not

to open. They knew that time was against them. It would surely rain soon.

They were not at all surprised to find Isaac outside the stable, grooming White Lightning.

"Can we speak with you for a moment?" Lassa asked him on approach.

Isaac shrugged his shoulders. "I suppose." He walked White Lightning across to the

paddock to let her run for a while. "What about?"

Lassa ignored his question, her eyes darting nervously from him to White Lightning,

across to Urton Hall, then back again to Isaac.

"Where's Mr Cruickshank?" she asked nervously.

Isaac's eyes narrowed. "Why do you want to know?"

"We need to ask a favour."

"Of him or of me?"

Lassa's face immediately became intense. "You."

Isaac regarded her dispassionately. "Yeah?" he said without any real interest.

"Yeah," Lydia confirmed at Lassa's side. She knew Isaac had always had a soft spot for

her, and thought now might be a good time to use that fact to her advantage. She tossed her l

long blonde hair flirtatiously over her graceful, shawled shoulders and flashed him her most dazzling smile. She moved forward slowly so that her face was level with his. "We really

need your help, Isaac."

Isaac swallowed visibly. His face flushed tomato-red and his eyes shined. "What - what

for?" he stammered.

"Tell us where Mr Cruickshank is first," Lassa repeated her earlier question.

Isaac looked nervous whenever Cruickshank's name was mentioned.

"Well, I really shouldn't be telling you this, but he went to London last night. There was a

card game at Almack's gaming club. High stakes apparently." He turned to Lydia. She

smiled beatifically at him and he turned away again, delightfully embarrassed. "I only know

because I heard him arguing with Mrs Cruickshank about it before he left. I wasn't eavesdropping, but she was crying so loud, I couldn't do anything but overhear. She begged

him not to go." He ran a hand through his hair. "He's not expected back until early this

afternoon." He made a piteous frightened face, then lowered his head and kicked at his heels.

"I really hope he won. And big too or I'll – "

Lassa and Lydia looked at each other unhappily. They knew what each other was thinking,

for they were both thinking the same thing. When Joseph Cruickshank lost at cards, he

probably took it out on young Isaac.

They regarded Isaac sadly.

" – I'll be the one to suffer for it," Isaac finished, confirming their thoughts. He pulled up

his baggy cotton shirt to expose his bruised ribs and swollen skin, discoloured with patches of

dark purple and blue.

Lassa and Lydia simultaneously sucked in their breath in horror. Lassa was having second

thoughts as to whether she should really be asking Isaac to help them. It was so risky for

him.

"So what's this favour you want me to do for you then?" he asked, tucking his shirt back

into his breeches.

Lassa cleared her throat. Everything was riding on Isaac agreeing to help. She knew she

had to use her best persuasive skills to win him over.

"I need you to get me some parchment and a quill," she said.

Lydia, sensing Isaac's uncertainty, took a hold of his hand. "Please Isaac."

Completely beguiled, Isaac nodded.

"I can do that," he said. He puffed his chest out like a wood pigeon and trotted off towards

Urton Hall.

When he was out of sight, Lydia threw back her head, raised her arms, shook her shawl,

and whooped with joy.

"We did it!" she exclaimed.

"Don't get too carried away, Lydia," Lassa told her. "We need him to agree to do one

more thing before we can get too excited. And I have a feeling that to enlist his help in our

next task will be much trickier."

She walked over to the stable door and peeked inside. The conker mare was stood in the

far corner, fetlock deep in straw, feeding her young foal. The bucket of soot wash that Lassa

had spotted on her first visit to Urton Hall was still present. She chewed on the inside of her cheek. It was all going to plan, so far. But her plan relied on Isaac agreeing to do something

far more dangerous than pocketing a sheet of parchment paper and a quill from Joseph

Cruickshank's bureau. But she would worry about that later.

Upon hearing Isaac's heavy returning footsteps, Lassa turned. He took a scroll of

parchment paper from under his arm. The scroll was small and tied with a blue ribbon. A

fine feathered quill was positioned securely behind his ear.

He staged a mock bow.

"There, I told you I could do it," he said proudly, flushed with success. He stole a glance

at Lydia, who winked at him obligingly. "Is that all you want me to do?" he asked as he

handed over the scroll and the quill to Lassa.

Lassa gave a quick nod. "For now," she said, taking the scroll. She instructed Lydia to turn around, rolled out the scroll and smoothed it down the length of her back with the palm

of her hand. Then she took up the quill and began to write.

Cruickshank,

Menzies is an innocent man. I know it and you know it too. I know

Dan Dandy's true identity and I have the evidence to prove it!

But my silence can be bought.

For a price.

Meet me at four o'clock

sharp on the stretch of road leading out of the village, at the exact

spot of Dan Dandy's last stage-coach robbery.

I assume you know where that is?

Of course you do, since you are, in fact, Dan Dandy!

Come alone.

Anon

Isaac craned his neck to peer over Lassa's shoulder.

"What are you writing?" he asked.

"A letter," Lassa replied shortly. She dotted her Is and crossed her Ts with a flourish, then

rolled up the scroll and retied it with the blue ribbon. She handed it to Isaac. "Make sure you

give this to Mr Cruickshank the very moment he returns home from London. Tell him

a gentleman asked you to give it to him, but you didn't recognise him and he didn't give his

name. Don't mention that either myself or Lydia have been here.

Isaac nodded mutely and took hold of one end of the outstretched scroll. Lassa did not release her grip on the other. She wanted to be sure that he appreciated the importance of

what she was asking him to do before relinquishing it to him.

"Give this to him the very moment he returns home," she repeated firmly. "The very

moment, d'you hear?"

Isaac looked affronted. "I may not be able to read or write like you can, Miss Clever

Clogs, but you don't have to repeat yourself. I understood you just fine the first time."

Lassa let go of the scroll.

"Very well then," she said. She looked across at Lydia, and with a discreet tilt of her

auburn-haired head, gestured for her to move away, out of earshot. She did not want her

hearing what she was about to ask Isaac to do next. Or what she intended saying in order to persuade him to do it.

Affronted, Lydia responded with a scowl and a flick of her head, then reluctantly sloped

off to the paddock to admire White Lightning, who was now grazing alongside a brown pony.

Isaac couldn't take his eyes off her.

Lassa read his thoughts. His obvious infatuation for Lydia would have him playing into

right her hands.

"She's very fond of you, you know," she told him in a low voice.

Isaac's eyes lit up at once.

"Really?" he said keenly. "I thought she was friendly with the miller's son, what's-his-

name - ?"

"Jacob. Jacob Campion."

"That's it!" he said, clicking his fingers in recognition of the name. "Is she not spoken for then?"

"Oh no," Lassa said coyly, her fingers crossed behind her back. "It's you she likes. In

fact, she wants me to arrange a meeting between the two of you."

Isaac looked across at Lydia again, who was standing next to White Lightning, running her

long, slender hands across the mare's face and glorious white mane.

"I'd sure like that," he cooed. "What time? Where?"

"This afternoon," Lassa said, hating herself for misleading him like this, but knowing that

it was all for the greater good. "Do you know the road that leads away from the village?"

Isaac nodded eagerly.

"She'll be on that road a little after four o'clock, about a quarter of a mile out."

Isaac exhaled a huge puff of air with barely concealed excitement. He could hardly believe his luck. “Super!” he said, beaming.

Lassa registered a fleeting look of guilt, but Isaac seemed oblivious to it as he nodded in

Lydia’s direction and ran a hand coquettishly through his hair when she happened to look his

way.

“Tell her I’ll be there,” he said, winking at Lydia, who unwittingly winked back.

Having succeeded in sweet-talking him, Lassa decided it was the right time to take the bull

by the horns and ask one final favour of him. She drew closer to him conspiratorially.

“Oh, and one more thing – ” she began.

Isaac was all ears.

*

"What did you say to him?" Lydia demanded to know as they began their walk down the

drive to leave Urton Hall behind them.

Lassa winked at her.

"You'll find out all in good time," she said surreptitiously.

Their next stop was Dr Calder's cottage, to speak with Mrs Clarissa Fairweather. For what

reason, Lydia did not know, nor did she feel that she needed to. She found herself quite

happy to place all of her faith in Lassa's young hands, trusting her, quite literally, with her

father's life.

She worried about her father desperately, incarcerated as he was in Newgate Prison, where

disease, hunger and violence were prevalent. And she missed him beyond all comprehension.

The house seemed empty without him and her mother was half a woman now that he was not

around for her. The last few days had been the worst of Lydia's life. Had it not been for

Lassa's unfailing support, hope and eternal optimism, she dared not imagine how she would

have coped.

Lydia considered that the Menzies had found a good friend indeed in Lassa Hope.

They found Mrs Fairweather in the garden of the cottage, picking flowers for Dr Calder's

drawing room. Pretty winter pansies filled her basket, as did lupins and full-bloomed

chrysanthemums. She looked up from the flowerbed as she heard them nearing and she

smiled.

"Hello girls," she said cheerily.

Having allowed herself a few days to recover from her ordeal at the hands of Dan Dandy, her disposition had much improved. Her cheeks had taken on a rosy, healthy glow and her

eyes were a sparkling azure blue. Lassa and Lydia couldn't help but to be taken aback by the

warmth in Clarissa's greeting. Considering that Lydia's father had been arrested as

being the notorious highwayman, Dan Dandy, of whom Clarissa herself had fallen victim, it

was a wonder she had acknowledged them at all.

They looked at each other in surprise.

"Hello, Mrs Fairweather," Lydia said, risking a smile.

Lassa echoed the greeting in a small voice, her eyes narrowed. She wondered why Mrs

Fairweather wasn't shooing them away. Surely she knew of Lydia's father's arrest?

Clarissa snapped a lupin from its bed and placed it carefully into her almost-full basket.

"If it's Dr Calder you're after, I'm afraid he's out running an errand at present," she

chirruped.

Lassa cleared her throat. "Actually, it was you we came to see."

"Oh?" Clarissa raised a quizzical eyebrow.

"We want you to help us prove that my father isn't Dan Dandy, that the wrong man has

been arrested!" Lydia blurted without warning.

Lassa glared at Lydia, but it was too late. The damage had been done.

Clarissa's smile immediately faded to be replaced with a frown and she staggered

backwards, with her hand on her chest, as though reeling from an invisible blow. Her basket

of flowers dropped to the ground with a thud, splaying flowers onto the earth.

"Your father has been arrested?" she cried out. Her bottom lip gave a wobble. "They

think he's Dan Dandy?"

Lassa tried to retrieve the situation before the gravity of the news fully sunk in and before

Clarissa's state of shock gave way to an outburst of anger and betrayal.

"But it's not true!" Lassa told her emphatically. "It's all a terrible mistake."

"Oh I already know that!" Clarissa chipped in to Lassa and Lydia's astonishment. "Moses

Menzies couldn't possibly be Dan Dandy. Those eyes - those evil, penetrating eyes - they

belonged to nobody I have ever met in social circles." She rounded on Lydia to regard her

squarely. "And I have met your father on many, many occasions."

Lassa and Lydia caught sight of Henry Fairweather bumbling towards them from the cottage. He looked anxious. Clarissa followed their gaze and threw her husband an

indignant state.

"Why didn't you tell me that Moses Menzies had been arrested? That they believe him to

be Dan Dandy?" she demanded to know. "The very notion is preposterous!"

Henry tried to placate his wife with a smile.

"My dear, you were so distraught after the robbery, and you have been so ill and

melancholy of late, that your brother and I thought it best not to trouble you with such

trifles."

"Trifles!" Clarissa looked at him askance. "Trifles! What absolute poppycock! They

could hang an innocent man! You know as well as I do that Moses Menzies could not

possibly be Dan Dandy!"

Henry gave an embarrassed cough. "But the evidence does seem irrefutable, my dear."

"But Lydia and I have evidence too, " Lassa chipped in. "Evidence that will prove

Mr Menzies to be completely innocent of all the charges laid against him." She turned to

Clarissa, her eyes pleading. "Please – please will you help us? We believe we know the real

face behind Dan Dandy's mask, but we need your help and - "

Clarissa smiled broadly.

"I will help in any way I can," she said, cutting Lassa off mid-sentence.

Behind her, Henry looked unsure.

"I really don't think we should get involved, my dear," he said, throwing Lassa and Lydia

an awkward glance.

Clarissa ignored him to retrieve her basket from the floor and Lassa and Lydia bent down

to help her collect the fallen flowers.

"What do you need me to do?"

Without hesitation, Lasa replied. "Be on the road that leads out of the village at four

o'clock. All will be revealed then."

Much to her husband's chagrin, Clarissa Haughton nodded.

Lassa beamed.

All that she required now was for Captain Bywater to also be on the road leading out of the

village at four o'clock and the stage would be set.

So far so good.

Provided the rain held off.

*

"Sir, you gave us one week to find conclusive proof of Mr Menzies' innocence," Lassa said

in the sitting room of Captain Bywater's home sometime later. "Well, we've got it."

Fortunately the rain had not fallen as it had threatened to and the skies had virtually

cleared, with just a hint of cloud cover over the distant hills.

With the weather in their favour, Lassa and Lydia had neither dillied nor dallied on their

way to see Captain Bywater, and now that they were here, talking with him, Lassa truly felt

for the first time that everything would turn out for the better.

Captain Bywater chewed thoughtfully on his bottom lip as he pondered Lassa's declaration

and deliberated how to phrase his thoughts into words.

"Miss Hope, may I remind you that I am a very busy man," he said. His eyes narrowed,

but he met Lassa's gaze evenly and spoke very calmly. "And whilst I would love to believe

that you have the proof to command Moses Menzies' release, I can – "

Lassa sprang immediately to her feet.

"You must give us a chance, you must!" she cried out, sensing that Captain Bywater was

about to dismiss their evidence without having even heard or seen it. "A man's life is at

stake!"

Captain Bywater's eyes darkened to a silvery coal colour and Lassa immediately regretted

her outburst.

"I apologise, sir," she said in a small voice, her head held low in shame. This was not how

her grandparents had brought her up. She retook her seat. "I forgot myself."

There was a brief silence. Lassa's eyes flickered up to meet the captain's and their gazes

held for a fleeting moment, the space of a heartbeat, before Captain Bywater's mouth

widened into a huge smile.

"You are a very determined young lady aren't you, Miss Hope?" he said. "I wish there

were more men like you in His Majesty's Navy with even half your grit, tenacity and

fortitude."

Lassa, still shamed, shifted in her chair and started to stammer. Her tongue tried to make

familiar sounds, but they wouldn't come.

Captain Bywater laughed and, in a gesture of defeat, held up both hands high in the air.

"I can spare you one hour," he said.

Lassa visibly relaxed and exhaled a long sigh. Lydia turned to her with a euphoric sile.

"We will need you from just before four o'clock," Lassa advised him cryptically.

Captain Bywater's face broke into an open smile, He plainly admired the red-headed

teenager. She was quite unique. He had never before met a child of such intellect, frankness

and steely determination, and he found himself believing in her.

"Call for me at a quarter to the hour," he directed her. "I will be ready for you then."

Lassa resisted the urge to jump up from her chair, to hug him and plant huge kisses

over his face and hands in thanks and gratitude. Her heart was as full as it had ever been.

Soon the nightmare would all be over for Lassa and the Menzies.

Moses would be coming home. She was certain of it.

Chapter Twelve

Newgate Prison

Moses lay motionless in a foetal position, with no cover and barely any clothes. Heavy

manacles constricted any movement he may have wished to make. They were shackled to his

arms and legs and were secured by chains and staples in the cold, stone floor. He was cold

and hungry, having survived on just bread and water for days, and his hair was long

and greasy and infested with head lice.

The grim room was dark and foul-smelling and disease was all around. Many of his

cellmates, approximately two hundred of them – men, women and children – lay in their own

filth, shivering with a high fever and moaning woefully in delirium. Others could be heard uttering the most dreadful profanities, blaspheming and cursing the Keepers. Some sang

psalms impiously, drunk on the cheap gin that was readily available.

Rats lived among them, feeding on the corpses and taking bites out of the living too weak

to shake them off.

It was a scene most miserable, barbarous and vile. Moses began to weep, as much for his

wife and children, who would be missing him, as for his own feelings of desolation and fear.

All hope of freedom had long since diminished.

Moses Menzies was a broken man.

Chapter Thirteen

The Road Leading Away From the Village

At a quarter to four Lassa and Lydia called for Captain Bywater who, as promised,

accompanied them on foot to the road leading away from the village.

The captain was dressed in his full Naval regalia of a full-skirted, dark blue dress coat with

no collar and deep boot cuffs, matching breeches with four brass buttons stitched at the knee,

die-stamped with the anchor motif, and a white wool waistcoat. So as to avoid displacement

of his wig and hair powder, under his arm he carried a three-cornered hat made of felt and

edged with silver lace. A long silver sword with a knuckle-guard hung from his sword belt

and glinted in the late afternoon sun to torch the ground with a soft, golden glow.

He looked very much the figure of authority and Lassa felt glad to have him on side.

She showed him the trench where she and Moses had hid the night of Dan Dandy's last

call to stand and deliver, and drew his attention to the many markings in the road. Lydia

remained silent at the road's edge, hoping that now, at long last, Lassa's fascination with

them would become clear to her.

"These – " - Lassa pointed to the long, narrow track marks in the moist earth - " - are the

tracks left by the carriage. And these – " - she pointed to the footprints - " - are the markings

left by the coachman and by his passenger, and also by Mr Menzies and Dan Dandy. The

men from the village too." She pulled a face. "As you can see they're all so badly

jumbled up, it would be hard to establish exactly which set of footprints belong to which

individual." She indicated to the paw prints of varying sizes. "And of course these are the markings left by the dogs. Tens of them there were, snarling and barking wildly."

The captain looked puzzled. "This is all very interesting, Miss Hope," he said finally with

an impatient sigh, "but I fail to see the relevance."

"You will," Lassa told him.

Lassa sank down to her haunches. The captain mirrored her action. On the ground in

between them, imbedded in the damp earth, was a clear set of hoof prints.

"Look at them closely," Lassa instructed him. "What do you see?"

The captain peered at them, and also at the trail of prints that continued further up the road,

merging a few feet away with the hoof prints of the two horses that had drawn the carriage.

He traced his fingers around their outline and observed with surprise that one print from each set of four was different somehow, less impacted than the other three, which were deep

and well defined.

"The horses that left these prints had one unshod hoof," he determined at length. "The

unshod hoof has met the ground in a different way to the others, since the horse was

obviously trying to evade the pain in the heel area, causing a more shallow and superficial

print."

Both Lassa and the captain remained crouched on the ground.

"Mr Joseph Cruickshank's horse, White Lightning, has one unshod hoof," Lassa revealed.

"Mr Cruickshank came to the smithy on the morning of Mr Menzies' arrest and asked Mr

Menzies to re-shoe her. Mr Menzies refused on account of the fact that Mr Cruickshank was unable, or unwilling, to settle an earlier bill of debt."

The captain rose to his feet.

"Miss Hope, are you suggesting that Mr Cruickshank is the man behind the mask of Dan

Dandy?" he asked incredulously.

Lassa stood. She struck out her nose obstinately and nodded her head.

"Yes, I am, sir," she said challengingly.

The captain gave a small laugh. "But that's ludicrous! Joseph is an upstanding member of

society. He is descended from the first Earl of Derby, who fought at the Battle of Bosworth."

He regarded Lassa in disbelief. "You are also forgetting that White Lightning's colour is as

pure a white as the driven snow. Dan Dandy's horse is white with black markings."

Lassa opened her mouth to respond, but the sound of an approaching horse silenced her.

"It's Mr Cruickshank," Lydia called to them. She was standing on tiptoes on a rock, her

hand blocking her eyes to the cold sunlight as she looked into the distance.

"What?!" The captain looked enraged. He turned to Lassa, his face thunderous. "Have

you requested his presence here? I cannot arrest the man on the strength of a few hoof

prints!"

"But there's more!" Lassa said urgently. "Sir, you have to believe me! Hide in the trench

and you will hear the truth for yourself."

The captain stared at her, unmoving, yet he felt strangely compelled to follow her order.

There was something about the freckle-faced little girl that commanded deference.

"Please!" Lassa implored, hearing the pounding of the approaching horse's hooves becoming louder and louder as it nearer closer.

"This is ridiculous," the captain was heard to mutter and yet, in spite of serious

reservations, he shook his head and took his place inside the trench.

Lassa and Lydia waited, their bodies stiff with anticipation.

Moments later Joseph Cruickshank came upon them. He halted his horse – the conker

mare – and slid down from her, reining her to the fence post.

"What are you doing here?" he demanded to know, clearly irritated.

"I was showing Lydia the place where her father was arrested", Lassa said.

Joseph Cruickshank glared at them both, his eyes chips of ice.

"Well now you've shown her, you can clear off!" he said in clipped tones.

Lassa stood stock still, overcome by the highly charged atmosphere and her anger towards the man that stood so pompously before her.

Joseph Cruickshank's growing fury was unmistakeable. His eyes bored down into Lassa's.

He was so close that she was made forcefully aware of everything about him: His angular

cheekbones, his pointed nose, piercing blue eyes and thin lips that were now beginning to

twist into an evil sneer.

Lassa turned, as though to walk away, but then stopped and turned back to say casually,

"By the way, what you said the other day about the tricorn hat with the initials JC...." Lassa

observed Joseph Cruickshank swallow hard, his Adam's apple bobbing in his throat. "I have

it under good authority that you bought your hat in August of last year, from the milliner in the village, Mr Darling, and so Dan Dandy could not possibly have stolen it from you, since

the robbery that you alleged took place is on record as having occurred sometime during the

month of the previous June."

Something inside Cruickshank snapped. He bared his teeth and started towards Lassa with

balled fists, his eyes dark and merciless. Only the sound of an advancing carriage prevented

him from turning his murderous thoughts into a reality. He stopped dead in his tracks and

swung around.

The coachman drew the carriage to a stop alongside him and outstepped Mrs Clarissa

Fairweather. She was accompanied by her reluctant husband, Henry.

Joseph Cruickshank looked momentarily flustered, but he quickly composed himself.

"Mr and Mrs Fairweather," he nodded in acknowledgement.

Henry raised an eyebrow.

"I'm afraid you have the advantage over me, sir, I don't believe we have met before." He

stretched out a hand and Joseph Cruickshank took a hold of it and shook it firmly.

Clarissa regarded Joseph Cruickshank warily. His whole manner made her feel

uncomfortable, although she could not think why. He seemed perfectly polite, charming

even, and yet there was something about him that unnerved her. He seemed familiar to her

somehow and yet she could not place having ever met him before.

Joseph Cruickshank looked baffled.

"I am Joseph Cruickshank," he said through narrowed eyes, without the courtesy of a

short, respectful head bow that was commonplace in the 1700s. "Am I to understand then, sir," he continued, "that it was not you that invited me to meet you here?"

He appeared distracted, looking about him nervously, and Lassa noticed that his brow was

damp with perspiration. She smiled. She had the man rankled. It was a small triumph.

Henry shook his head, mystified.

It was Clarissa that answered his question.

"We are here of our own volition, sir," she lied. "We heard that the views from this stretch

of road are quite stunning."

Joseph Cruickshank adopted a scathing expression as he regarded the mud track, barren

land, the surrounding bare trees and bracken.

"Quite," he said unconvincingly. He withdrew a fob watch from his dress coat pocket and glanced at the time. It was five minutes past the hour. "It seems I have been sent on a fool's

errand," he muttered to himself. He gave a heavy sigh. Then, turning to Henry, he said, "I

must take my leave of you, sir." He gave a curt nod of his head. "Mrs Fairweather."

Another nod, indicating his pending departure. "I'm afraid I have been called here under

false pretences and now I am late for another appointment."

Just as he turned to unleash the conker mare from the fence post, Isaac came into view. He

was walking towards the small party of people from a little way down the road, leading a

white horse with black markings alongside him. He was carrying a wooden bucket in his

hand and water was spilling out over the edge, falling in rivulets down the sides.

When he caught sight of Joseph Cruickshank he turned ashen faced and stopped dead in

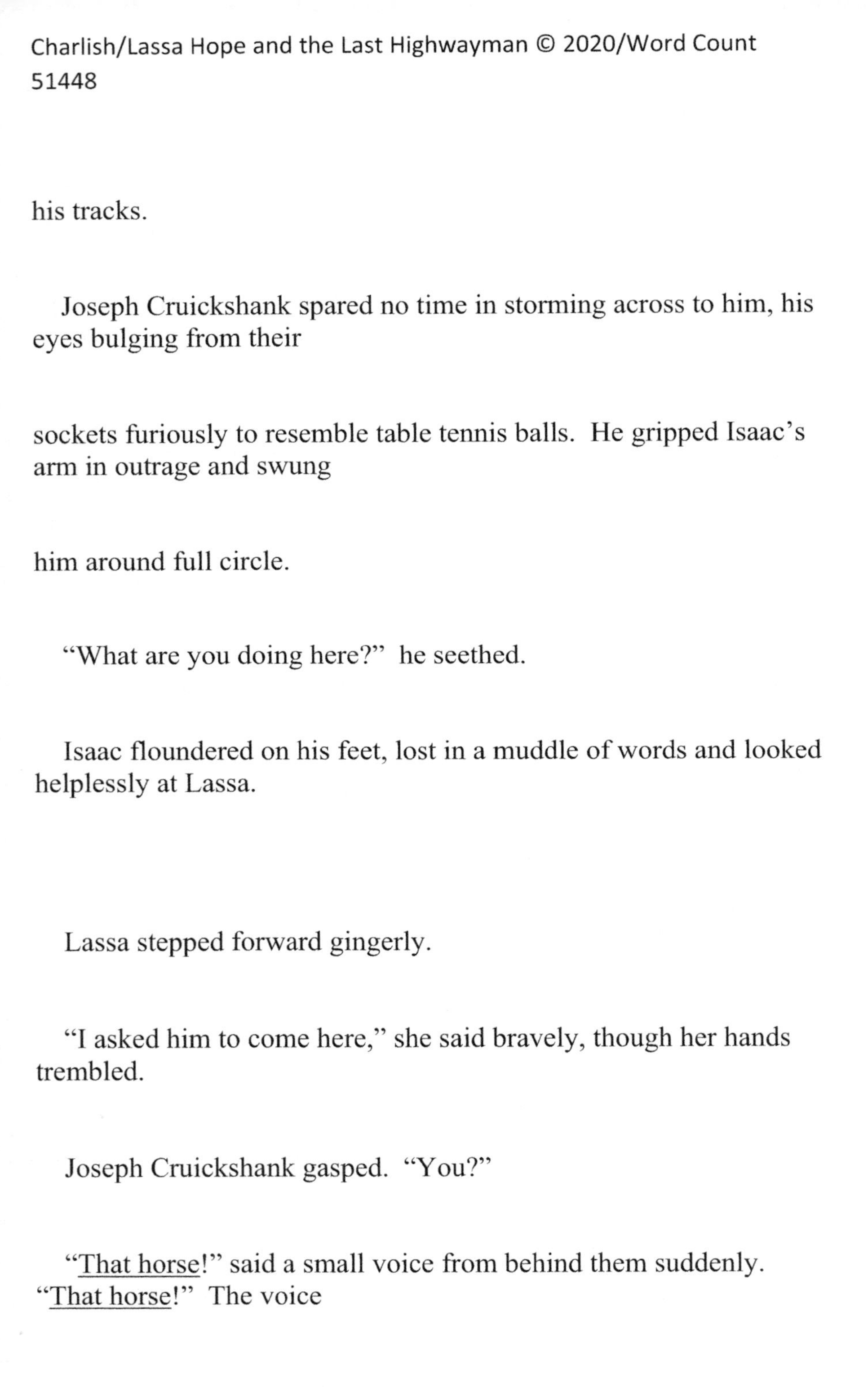

his tracks.

Joseph Cruickshank spared no time in storming across to him, his eyes bulging from their

sockets furiously to resemble table tennis balls. He gripped Isaac's arm in outrage and swung

him around full circle.

"What are you doing here?" he seethed.

Isaac floundered on his feet, lost in a muddle of words and looked helplessly at Lassa.

Lassa stepped forward gingerly.

"I asked him to come here," she said bravely, though her hands trembled.

Joseph Cruickshank gasped. "You?"

"That horse!" said a small voice from behind them suddenly. "That horse!" The voice grew progressively louder and louder. It was Clarissa's voice, now at shrieking pitch. "That horse is the one the highwayman rode the night Henry and I were robbed!"

Lassa, Joseph Cruickshank and Isaac turned simultaneously to find Clarissa Fairweather being supported by her husband. She was weeping softly into his chest and he was patting her back comfortingly.

"My wife is not wrong. That is the horse!" Henry confirmed stiffly. "To whom does it belong?"

"I haven't the faintest idea," replied Joseph Cruickshank briskly, looking agitated and sweating profusely. He flashed Isaac a warning glance and Isaac shuddered. Joseph Cruickshank cleared his throat. "I have never seen it before in my life," he continued in brusque tones.

"Is that so?" Lassa derided. "Tell me, Mr Cruickshank, why did you not come here on

White Lightning this afternoon?" Her blue eyes traded hard stares with the man before her.

His body was coiled like a cobra's, ready to spring at any moment. "She is your favourite

mare, is she not?"

Joseph Cruickshank visibly bristled at the question, but said nothing.

Lassa smiled slowly and her eyes crinkled cynically.

"Perhaps you could not find her," she said matter-of-factly. Isaac looked sheepish. Joseph

Cruickshank bared his teeth.

"I don't have time to stand here engaged in dialogue with <u>a child</u>," he spat.

He was about to mount his horse when he saw Lassa reaching inside Isaac's bucket to pull

out a wet rag. His eyes widened in alarm.

"Or perhaps this horse is White Lightening!"

Lassa wrung out the wet rag and proceeded to rub it onto the hind leg of the horse Isaac

held by the reins. The horse whinnied in protest and her hooves beat an irked tattoo on the

road. Instinctively Lassa reached out her hands to quieten her, stroking her, soothing her, as

she continued to rub at her coat.

There was gasps from all around as the black markings began to fade, then slowly, but

surely, disappeared without a trace to reveal the pure white coat of White Lightning beneath.

Clarissa's colour paled by such a degree that Lassa feared she might faint.

"Now I know why you are so familiar to me," she hissed to Joseph Cruickshank between sobs. Her legs were weak at the knees and had she not borne her weight upon her husband

she would have most certainly tumbled to the ground in a heap of cotton and fine lace.

"You are Dan Dandy, the man that robbed us! I recognise your eyes, so darkly unpleasant."

Joseph Cruickshank waved a dismissive hand. "Madam, this proves nothing."

From the trench Captain Bywater appeared. Lassa had almost forgotten about him.

Upon seeing the captain, the sneer slid off Joseph Cruickshank's face at an amazing speed

and his face paled to a ghastly hue. It suddenly dawned on him that he had been the victim

of entrapment. He licked at his suddenly dry, cracked lips.

The captain's long Naval dress coat danced behind him like a cape, snapping in the breeze

with each step as he moved towards Joseph Cruickshank, his expression unreadable.

"There are markings on the road that suggest that the highwayman's horse had one unshod

hoof," the captain said calmly. "Markings I believe that will match one of the hooves of this

white mare, which I believe belongs to you."

Overhead, clouds amassed, threatening rain. A chilly breeze raged across the road, lifting

dry leaves and bracken into the wind and tossing it several feet up the road. There was a

sudden flash of lightning followed closely by the crash of thunder, a demonic interruption of

the events on the road.

To gasps of horror, Joseph Cruickshank swiftly reached his left hand inside his dress coat

pocket and withdrew a pistol. In response, Captain Bywater drew the first inch of his sword.

"Don't be a fool, sir," Captain Bywater said, drawing his sword half way out. "Put the

pistol down."

Joseph Cruickshank cocked the pistol and aimed it straight at Captain Bywater's chest.

"Make me," he said.

Captain Bywater stared him dead in the eye. He neither cursed the villain nor pleaded for

his mercy, instead appearing to accept his fate with a dignity and poise that was synonymous

with his rank. Lassa held her breath and clung to Lydia, who was trembling and

whimpering.

Joseph Cruickshank's lips curled into a malevolent smile and his devilled eyes flashed

satanically. He pulled at the trigger.

Lassa squeezed her eyes tightly shut. Beside her Lydia gasped, her whole body stiffening as she braced herself for the inevitable.

The pistol misfired.

Clarissa almost swooned in Henry's arms. He hastened her into the carriage. Lydia clung

to Lassa and battled a wave of nausea. Isaac took three large steps backwards and cowered

behind White Lightning's flanks.

Joseph Cruickshank looked down the barrel in shock.

Lassa and Lydia visibly relaxed.

Captain Bywater drew his sword all the way out and set himself, taking two rapid steps

forwards. Joseph Cruickshank tried to back off, but was wrong footed by Captain Bywater's

advance and he feel to the ground. The pistol went airborne.

Captain Bywater grabbed him by his coattails and hoisted him to his feet. Joseph

Cruickshank swung round and slammed his fist into the side of the captain's face. Without

registering any concern, the captain returned the punch. Joseph Cruickshank was floored

once again, badly winded, gasping and gulping for air, a stream of blood trickling from his

lip to his chin.

He looked up at Captain Bywater from where he lay and smiled ruefully, roughly wiping

away the blood with the back of his hand. He rose to his feet unaided.

Captain Bywater gripped him by the top of his arms and this time, Joseph Cruickshank

made no attempt to struggle free. He turned to face Lassa, cocking his head to one side as he

spoke.

"How did you know?" he asked her.

Lassa felt her heart pound and her throat became dry but to her amazement her words came

out normally.

"Well – " She held up her hand and used her fingers to count off the points. One: The

tricorn hat with the initials JC. You admitted yourself that the hat Mr Menzies was wearing

on the night of his arrest could have been yours because it had been allegedly stolen from you

in a highway robbery that you claimed took place in June of last year. That just didn't tally

because you didn't even buy the hat until the following August. I know, because I saw the

sales ledger belonging to Mr Darling, the milliner. And so I came to the conclusion that you

never were the victim of a highway robbery; you concocted that story in an attempt to steer

suspicion away from you. Mr Menzies was only wearing your hat that night because you placed it on his head while he was out cold. Two: I knew that Dan Dandy's horse was white,

with distinctive black markings. I put two and two together when I saw the bucket of soot

wash in your stables. You would simply disguise her to make her look like a completely

different horse. Three: The markings on the road here indicate that Dan Dandy's horse had

one unshod hoof. White Lightning has an unshod hoof. I know, because as you will

remember, I was at the blacksmith's shop on the day you asked Mr Menzies to re-shoe

her. He refused. And also – " - she paused, wondering if she was pushing her luck -

" - when you took up your quill to write Mr Menzies a promissory note, I notice that you

were left-handed."

Joseph Cruickshank raised a quizzical brow. "So?"

"I recollect Mrs Fairweather re-enacting the robbery. She used her left hand to

demonstrate how the highwayman – you – wielded his pistol. She also observed that the

highwayman had a small scar on his pistol finger."

Captain Bywater tore the riding glove from Joseph Cruickshank's left hand and discarded

it on the ground. Sure enough, on his pistol finger, between his knuckle and his nail, there

was a red and angry-looking one-inch scar.

Joseph Cruickshank sighed and rubbed at the scar penitently.

"I lost at cards," he said ruefully. "I was so mad I crushed a wine flute in my hand.

Darned thing bled for hours."

With his shoulders hunched over and his head held low, Lassa found herself feeling almost sorry for him. He was now counting the cost of losing at cards once too often. Crippled by

gambling debts, he had turned to a life of crime. And due to the inefficiency and inaptitude

of the authorities, he had evaded arrest for more than a year, carrying out robbery after

robbery with undeniable flair.

But his life of crime was now at an end, brought about by one clever and courageous little

girl.

In Lassa Hope, Joseph Cruickshank had met his match.

"Would it help to say I'm sorry?" Joseph Cruickshank asked lamely.

Lassa said nothing. Lydia deliberately looked away.

Captain Bywater knocked on the carriage door and Henry Fairweather opened it cautiously

from the inside. He was concerned for his wife, that much was plain. His brow was etched with anxiety.

"I beg your pardon, sir," said the captain. He ripped the curtain sash from the carriage

window and used it to truss Joseph Cruickshank's wrists together behind him. He snapped

the carriage door shut and moved back, calling up to the coachman. "Sir, take the

Fairweathers back to Dr Calder's cottage. And do not spare the horses! I fear Mrs

Fairweather has had a nasty shock."

The relieved looking coachman cracked his whip and the horses broke into a canter,

towing away the carriage at speed.

Captain Bywater twisted himself around to face Lassa and Lydia.

"Ladies, I must take my leave of you."

Lassa looked up at him, her eyes sparkling, both with gratitude and unshed tears.

"Thank you, sir," she said. "For believing in me."

"Yes, thank you sir," said Lydia. Her bottom lip trembled and her eyes spilled over with

tears of relief. "For giving us the chance to prove what we knew to be true all along, that my

father was a wronged man."

The captain doffed his hat, clicked his heels together in a parting salute and proceeded to

make haste along the road back to towards the village, escorting the bound and emotionally

beaten Joseph Cruickshank at his side.

Lassa and Lydia stared after them, watching them become smaller as they disappeared up

the road. When they were finally out of sight, they looked not up at the road, but at each other. Their expressions mirrored each other's. It was one of complete and utter elation.

Lydia wrapped her arms around Lassa and whooped with joy. And together they jumped up

and down on the spot, clinging to each other, laughing through tears of happiness.

They would have continued celebrating until it grew dark had Isaac not appeared at their

side, coughing and hemming to face Lydia with bewilderment.

"Um – I – um – I was told you wanted to meet me here." His words came out in a tumble.

"I was told you wanted to ride with me upon White Lightning, but that it would be best to

mark her with soot wash so as to disguise her, so that word wouldn't reach Mr Cruickshank

to say that I had been larking about on his mare." He threw a puzzled look down at the

wooden water bucket he still carried at his side. "I'm not quite sure why Lassa told me to bring this."

Lydia flew at Lassa in mock outrage and together they spluttered with laughter.

Isaac looked confused.

"I risked everything to be here," he groused.

Lydia, still laughing, rewarded Isaac with a kiss on the cheek and encircled him in her

arms. Her laughter was infectious; before long all three of them were rolling about at the side

of the road, gripping their sides with mirth.

It was a happy day indeed.

Chapter Fourteen

A Great Celebration

By the time Lassa and Lydia arrived home, word of Joseph Cruickshank's arrest had already

met Mary. Dr Calder had called round with the good news immediately upon hearing it

himself from Henry and Clarissa, who had recounted to him the afternoon's events without

barely stopping to breathe.

"Lydia! Lassa!" Mary cried out from the sitting room as the front door was pushed open.

"Is that you?"

She met them in corridor, shaking with emotion, daring not to believe what she had been

told to be true until she had heard it from her own daughter's mouth.

"Tell me it's over, Lydia," she said, her voice faltering with nervous tension. "Tell me my

Moses is coming home."

Lydia collapsed into her mother's arms, sobbing tears of joy.

"It's over, mother," she affirmed, smiling widely. "Father's coming home."

They clung to each other for what seemed like an eternity, laughing and crying at the same

time. Lassa moved towards them and was encircled at once. Mary rained kisses all over her

face and hands, thanking her over and over again, blessing her and praising the Lord.

"It's a miracle!"" she declared through her tears. "Nothing short of a miracle!"

Philomena entered into the corridor with Esme and twins in tow. She was smiling broadly

from ear to ear.

"Buckles and Bootlaces, Lassa!" she said, throwing her arms around her to give her as big

a squeeze as her aching bones would permit. "Well done!" She congratulated her. "You have achieved exactly what you set out to do."

The twins, Elizabeth and Temperance, clung to Lassa's skirt tails and looked up in hero

worship.

"You saved our father!" they declared in chorus.

"You are an angel sent from God," Mary added. She went over to Lassa and planted a kiss

on her freckled forehead. "Thank you," she said in a steady voice. "Thank you – from all of

us – for everything."

As she regarded the faces before her, each one a picture of utter jubilation, Lassa felt so

happy she thought her heart would burst.

Mary, Lydia, Esme and the twins formed a chain and began to dance gaily around the room, laughing and singing merrily. It was as though the world had started to spin on its axis

once more, and normality had at last been restored.

Lassa and Philomena exchanged meaningful glances. They both knew that this signalled

the end.

In spite of her happiness, Lassa felt suddenly saddened. In just a few short days the

Menzies had come to mean a great deal to her. She knew she would never forget them, not

for as long as she lived. But soon she and the Professor would be having to say their

goodbyes, for it was now time to go home.

Lydia grabbed Lassa by the hand to join the chain and together they snaked around the

room. Philomena took a seat and clapped in time with the singing.

It was a dance of celebration that lasted over half an hour, until they all fell exhausted onto the floor, red-faced and panting, in a sea of petticoats.

The news of Moses Menzies' pending release spread fast and furiously throughout the

village, and one well-wisher after the other arrived at the cottage, bearing gifts of meats,

cheeses, fruits and bread loaves. Dick Maynard, landlord at The Staff and Shepherd, called

round with a barrel of mead, and Jacob Campion and his father arrived with their fiddles to

whip up an impromptu party that lasted well into the early hours of the morning. Everyone

sang and danced with real joy, for it was a rare excuse for a celebration, and a welcome relief

from the daily toil and struggle.

Lassa's head did not hit the pillow until the sun was rising to bring in the new day.

Chapter Fifteen

Free

Captain Bywater delivered his credentials to the turnkey who answered his knock at the

imposing black door of Newgate Prison, which was heavily bound with iron and studded with

nails. Presently, he was ushered into the Governor's office, occupied by three clerks and

accommodating a wainscoted partition, a desk, tow chairs, a bookcase and a few wooden

stools.

A Keeper was sent for, a man in his early forties dressed in a full suit of black, and Captain

Bywater was escorted without further delay along a grim stone passageway and through

countless torturous and intricate windings, each one guarded by a huge gate with gratings, its portentous appearance sufficient to dispel immediately the slightest hope of escape that any

new arrival may have entertained.

At the end of one such unlit winding corridor, there was a large room full of men, women

and children, bound and helpless, their hours numbered, and from whom any small ray of

hope had long since taken flight.

Captain Bywater required the Keeper to point Moses Menzies out to him, for he was so

borne down in body and soul by misery and desolation that he was utterly unrecognisable to

him.

He lay asleep on the floor, restrained with ponderous irons; four rings connected by chains

upon each arm and leg. He was unshaven, wore no clothes of any consequence, and he was

shivering as though suffering from a fever.

"Mr Menzies?" Captain Bywater said softly, nudging Moses gently awake. "Mr Menzies,

I have come to take you home."

Captain Bywater turned to the Keeper.

"This man requires urgent medical attention, I must get him out of here."

The Keeper nodded soberly and together they hauled Moses to his feet.

Unlike any of the other wretched souls around him, Moses was just minutes away from

freedom.

Chapter Sixteen

Fond Farewells

Lassa awoke just before noon. The sun was streaming in at the window. There was no wind

and absolute stillness prevailed.

Lydia popped her head round Lassa's door to invite her down for a bite to eat, but on

learning that it was salt fish and parsnip bread – did Mary know of no other vegetable? –

Lassa declined, feigning illness.

"Too much excitement yesterday, I do declare," Lydia said happily.

She ventured slowly into Lassa's room.

"Mrs Dovetail has told my mother that you will be leaving today," she said, her face having suddenly adopted a more sullen expression.

Lassa rose from the bed and walked over to where Lydia was standing to embrace her

warmly in her arms.

"We have been away long enough," she said gently. "It's time to go home."

Lydia nodded in stoic understanding.

"Thank you for looking after my aunt," Lassa continued. Her voice was full of gratitude

and warmth. "I have never known such kindness in strangers."

Lydia smiled a little shyly.

"Strangers no more though, eh?" she said, elbowing Lassa playfully.

Lassa laid a gentle hand on Lydia's arm.

"Strangers no more," she confirmed with gladness, realising that Lydia was her first ever real friend outside of her grandparents and the Professor.

A door slamming echoed around the walls of the cottage and the sound of Mary's voice,

raised high with emotion, reverberated throughout.

Lassa and Lydia jumped in surprise and froze, neither daring to move.

And then, just moments later, the sound of Esme and the twins' elated cries wafted into the

room.

Lydia's eyes blinked and shone.

"It's my father!" she breathed.

She dashed excitedly out of the room and ran downstairs, taking two steps at a time in her

impatience to reach him. Lassa was hot on her heels.

Moses Menzies stood at the foot of the stairs. He was thin and gaunt looking, but otherwise he was unchanged. His smile was wide, his arms open and outstretched before

him.

Without ceremony, Lydia threw herself at him, flinging her arms around his body,

clutching on to him so tightly that Lassa feared she would squeeze all the air from his lungs.

He swooped her up and swung her round, dancing her around the corridor, crushing her so

close to him that she could feel his heart beating. Lydia never wanted to let him go.

Moses stopped dancing her around and held her close.

"Oh Lydia, how I missed you!" he declared. He had dark rings under his eyes and his

cheeks were hollow through lack of food. "I thought I would never see you again. I didn't

think I would see any of you again," he said, pausing to look at his wife and each of his four daughters in turn. "I feared this day would never come. I had almost lost all hope."

Standing at his side, her face stained with tears of joy, Mary nodded her head halfway up

the staircase, to where Lassa stood watching silently over them, misty-eyed. Philomena stood

two steps above her. She too was moved by the happy reunion and her throat was sore and

tight with the effort it took to thwart the onset of tears.

Moses' eyes followed his wife's line of vision and he smiled.

"Lassa," he said. "Words are not enough – " His voice broke with emotion. He bit his

bottom lip, tears welling in his eyes.

Mary reached out and set a hand on his arm, sensing that he was overcome with the depth

of his gratitude. She passed him a look that said she would speak for him. She took a deep breath.

"What my husband is trying to say, very inarticulately," she said in choked tones. "Is that

we will never be able to repay you for what you have done for us."

Lassa looked embarrassed.

"You're very welcome, " she said, overwhelmed.

Behind her, Philomena cut short any further converse.

"I'm afraid we really must leave now," she said regretfully. "We have been away from

home for far too long. We will have been missed." She took two steps down, so that she was

on a level with Lassa. She took her hand. "But I speak for both of us when I say that we

have been very grateful for your hospitality."

Together, Lassa and Philomena walked down the last four steps of the staircase.

"It's been an absolute pleasure," Mary said sincerely, hugging both of them in turn.

"Promise you'll come visit us?"

Lassa was discomfited, a feeling made all the more acute by the hopeful expressions that

were turned on her.

"Maybe. One day," she confirmed, with Philomena nodding in agreement at her side.

And so, just an hour later, Lassa and Philomena found themselves bidding goodbye to their

new friends, their sadness only slightly tempered by the knowledge that they were returning

home, to their own time.

"Are you sure I can't escort you into the village?" Moses asked them for the umpteenth

time as they were saying their final farewells outside the cottage.

"Thank you, no," Philomena said. "We shall take our leave of you here. Stay with your

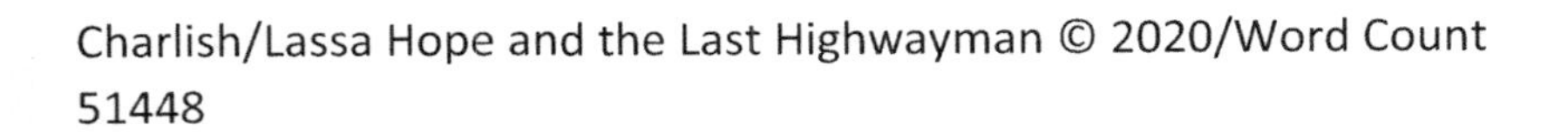

family, they have missed you so very much."

Moses bowed his head.

"As you wish, Mrs Dovetail," he said.

Beside him, Mary took a sharp intake of breath and a big fat tear escaped her eye and

rolled unchecked down her cheek.

"Goodbye Lassa," she said, encircling her in her arms. "Take very good care of yourself."

She embraced Philomena. "Goodbye, Mrs Dovetail."

Lydia came forward with a posy of flowers with white blossoms. To make the bunch

complete she bent down to pluck some rich blue, leafy rosettes from their bed, bound them

together, and then gave the whole bunch to Lassa, saying simply, "They're called Forget-Me-

Nots."

Lassa received them gratefully.

"Thank you," Her voice cracked and her lips quivered. She hugged Lydia for one last

time, then steeled her resolve and released her. "Goodbye, my dear friend."

She and Philomena kissed Esme and the twins and then they left, waving all the way as

they walked down the leafy lane, even once the Menzies and their chocolate-box cottage was

well out of sight.

With the tearful farewells behind them, Lassa and Philomena now only looked forward,

concentrating on stopping the tears from flowing and focusing on what awaited them back

home, in their own time.

Chapter Seventeen

Back to the Future

Lassa and Philomena made their way to Mr Groombridge's barn in contemplative silence.

Both were worried about what awaited them back in their own time How would they be able

to explain away their absence? What questions would they be required to answer? And how

on earth would they answer them? Thoughts and concerns tumbled through their minds, one

after the other in hasty succession.

"What will I say to my grandparents?" Lassa said, her voice racked high with nerves despite her sudden growing excitement at the prospect of seeing them again. "They will have

been so worried!"

"And what will I say to the Headmaster?" Philomena said, not so excited at the prospect of

seeing him again, with his beady little eyes and short temper. She exhaled. "Not to mention

the authorities. What will they think of me, disappearing with a child?" She patted Lassa on

the shoulder. "No matter, we'll muddle through it all somehow. The important thing is,

we'll be home."

They came upon Mr Groombridge's barn in the clearing and entered inside tentatively. It

was empty. Lassa retrieved her school rucksack from behind the haystack in the corner and reached inside for the clothes she had stuffed in there what now seemed like a million years

ago. They emerged wrinkled.

"They're terribly creased," she complained, screwing up her face at the sight of her school

blouse.

"Yes," agreed Philomena, regarding her own clothes with disdain.

"Still, what does it matter?" Lassa said with a shrug. "I'm sure a few creases never killed

anyone and I will challenge anyone who tells me otherwise!"

"Buckles and bootlaces! How you have changed these past few days!" Philomena

declared. She winked at Lassa indulgently. "I trust you will use some of this new-found

confidence when we're back home," she said with a meaningful look.

Lassa nodded, her thoughts turning to Clare Fox for the first time in days. She gave an involuntary shiver. After all she had been through, she feared she could still be intimidated

by her if she allowed herself to be.

"The worm has turned, Professor," Lassa assured her as she tied her shoe-laces into a bow.

She shook her hair free from her muslin cap and it spilled over her shoulders to resemble a

red waterfall. "I refuse to put up with her bullying any longer. I have to make a stand. I

know I can. I am much stronger now."

Philomena snaked an arm around Lassa's shoulders and pulled her close to kiss the top of

her head.

"That's the spirit," she said. She made a vain attempt to smooth away the creases in her

white blouse. "Ready?"

Lassa nodded.

"As ready as I'll ever be," she said cheerfully, carefully placing the Forget-Me-Nots Lydia

had given her into the outer sleeve of her school rucksack. "Let's go."

She hauled her rucksack over her shoulders and followed Philomena stealthily out of the

barn.

The portal was exactly where Lassa and Philomena had expected to find it, despite the

cross of sticks having virtually disappeared in the recent high winds and torrential rains.

Lassa threw her rucksack up into it and it was immediately banished, the shimmering circle

flinching only slightly with the force of the impact.

"It still seems to be functioning," Lassa said.

"Did you have any doubts?" Philomena asked.

Lassa shrugged.

"The thought had crossed my mind that we could end up being stuck here forever."

Philomena gave a little laugh.

"That thought had crossed my mind too," she admitted. She looked around. "Well, take

once last look, Lassa. We'll never see this place again."

Taking one last lingering look, Lassa thrust herself through the portal without trepidation

to appear, head and shoulders, in the 21st Century classroom she had last seen almost a

week ago.

The room was empty and seemingly unchanged. The whiteboard still had the same

chemical equations scrawled onto it as when she had last seen it. The handwriting was

without a doubt the Professor's. It was almost indecipherable. Indeed, Lassa thought the marks could just have easily have been made by a rheumatic money spider wearing black ink

boots as it darted across from one side of the board to the other.

There was a tripod on its side on the floor beside her and a Bunsen Burner still flickered on

Philomena's wooden desk. More tellingly, the large LED calendar wall-clock at the back of

the room read: 10:35 Monday April 22nd 2019.

Whilst Lassa and Philomena were in 18th Century England saving Moses Menzies from the

hangman's noose, time had stood virtually still.

Lassa heaved herself through the portal fully and called to Philomena to follow on after

her. Philomena wriggled through moments later. She looked around the room, wide-eyed

and startled.

"Buckles and bootlaces! It's exactly how we left it," she said, scarcely able to believe her eyes. "It's as though time has stood still. We won't have been missed at all!"

There was a sudden noise from behind; a strange unfamiliar slurping sound, the kind a giant slug would make as it dragged its sticky body across a plastic surface.

Lassa and Philomena turned to see the portal diminishing slowly, receding inwards, and within seconds, it had completely disappeared. The floor was concrete once more and there was no evidence that it had actually ever been anything else.

Lassa's heart felt strangely heavy in her chest.

"Well that's that then," she said flatly.

"There's certainly no going back now," Philomena said.

"No," said Lassa soberly.

There was a knock at the classroom door and both Lassa and Philomena jumped out of

their skins in surprise. Mr Corrigan, the Headmaster, popped his head round.

"Ah, Professor Dovetail, may I have a quick word with you about next week's field trip to

the British Science Museum? It seems the coach can only seat 36 passengers and we have 38

students wanting to go."

Philomena appeared momentarily disconcerted.

"Ah yes, of course," she said, evidently flustered.

"And what on earth have you done to yourself? Your face is covered in bruises."

Mr Corrigan looked horrified, his beady eyes narrowed suspiciously. "Have you been doing

one of your silly experiments again?"

"I tripped over this morning in my rush to get to work," she told him regretfully. "I really

should take more care."

Mr Corrigan tutted.

"Yes, you must," he told her. He glanced at Lassa for the first time. "Run along to your

next lesson, the Professor and I have a problem to resolve."

Lassa hoiked her rucksack over her shoulder and turned to the Professor. "See you later,

Professor, thanks for everything."

Philomena pushed her slipping spectacles farther up her nose.

"It was – " She paused to choose her words carefully. "Interesting," she said at length.

"I had the time of my life, Professor," she revealed in a low voice.

Philomena winked and her spectacles fell promptly down her nose again. She looked over

them as she spoke.

"I have a feeling it won't be our last adventure, Lassa," she said sagely.

Lassa smiled widely. She hoped the Professor was right.

Chapter Eighteen

Lassa Makes a Stand

Uncharacteristically, Lassa decided to skip the next lesson, instead going to the school

library, which was located in the Humanities block.

It was vast and well stocked, largely with books to support the National curriculum and

literacy hour, but there was also an area dedicated to CDs and DVDs, and there were

shelves lined with general fiction and books of local interest.

It was the latter that was of significant importance to Lassa, and in particular a book she

had read many times in the past entitled Staffordshire: A Glimpse Through Time by Erica

Maddison. It was in this book that she had first learned of Moses Menzies being the last man

to have been gibbeted on Gibbet Hill. She was keen to read whether or not he got a mention now. After all, her actions had changed history. Hadn't they?

She found the book quite easily, on the third shelf in between Staffordshire, AA Map of the

Road and Staffordshire Bull Terriers, Man's Best Friend. It was old and dog eared.

Lassa took a seat on a footstool and began to leaf through the pages. She held her breath.

Somewhere towards the end of the thick book, she came across the section she had hoped to

find, under the heading of 18th Century Highways.

She swallowed hard and began to read it quietly to herself.

Highways were in relatively good shape in the 18th Century, despite the lack of

foundations, although the pressure of hooves and wheels caused them to become wet and

potholed in the winter months, and dusty and rutted in summer.

One traveller between Stone and Stoke, Dr John Calder, remarked in 1767 that he went

not through bogs and mires, but across land so smooth that [he] was able to travel at

remarkable pace and reached [his] journey's end twenty minutes ahead of schedule.

Lassa read on:

Of course Staffordshire's roads were never so troublesome or dangerous as they were

for a twelve month period between 1764 and 1765, during the reign of the notorious and

flamboyant highwayman, Joseph Cruickshank, a man of good family, whose exploits earned

him the nickname of Dan Dandy.

Riddled with gambling debts, Cruickshank took to the highways upon his horse, White

Lightning, and began terrorising travellers into surrendering their valuables to him. One of

his victims gamely resisted all efforts to rob him and he almost died in the struggle.

Lassa sat bolt upright. The text had changed from when she had last read the passage. Then

it had described Moses Menzies as the man who had terrorised the highways, and had given

an account of his execution and subsequent gibbeting on Gibbet Hill.

History had indeed been altered.

Cruickshank had achieved such notoriety that a bounty of £100 was placed on his head.

This reward was eventually claimed by a local blacksmith's family.

Lassa smiled to himself.

Due to the wealth and influence of his father, Joseph Cruickshank escaped the

hangman's noose and instead his sentence was commuted to transportation to a penal colony

in the Americas.

At his trial, Royal Naval officer, Captain Marcus Bywater, said, "I wish it to be known

that this felon will be forever excluded from all hope of return."

Lassa looked up from the book briefly and stared into space, immersed in deep thought. She

found herself feeling almost sorry for Joseph Cruickshank, that a man of his high standing

and privilege could have fallen so hard. With a heavy sigh, she turned her attention back to

the book.

However, despite surviving the long journey, Cruickshank died just two years after arrival in the Americas, his mental and physical health having succumbed to the interminable hard

labour, compounded by a poor diet and the dirty and overcrowded living conditions to which

he was not accustomed.

To this day, the leg irons which held Cruickshank whilst awaiting trial in Newgate Prison

can be seen in The Crime Museum located at New Scotland Yard in London.

Lassa felt herself stiffen, knowing that she had brought about this untimely end. Her measure

of guilt was assuaged only by the fact that in doing so, she had saved an innocent man's life.

Her conscience was sharpened, but in her heart of heart she knew that she had done the

right thing.

As she flicked further through the pages of the book, a second heading struck her:

Education and Schooling. She proceeded to read the text.

Gibbet Hill Secondary School and Community College, located on Blackberry Lane,

Tamworth, was built in 1975 on the site where a gibbet once stood, hence its name.

The last man to be gibbeted there was Samuel Jobling, mail robber and triple murderer.

Jobling was hanged on 12th March 1763. Three days later his body was brought to Gibbet

Hill. It is estimated that five thousand people visited the hill that day to oversee the

gruesome spectacle. Records state that in 1805, Jobling's ragged clothes and bones could

still be visible through the bars of the open cage. The gibbet was finally taken down in 1812,

when the new owner of the field where it stood complained of overzealous sightseers trespassing on his property and trampling his land.

Thankfully, there was no mention of Moses Menzies. Lassa snapped the book shut. She had

read enough. Many of the passages within the book she had read on many occasions in the

past had been altered, as had history itself.

She collected her things together and left the library.

It was almost noon now. Ordinarily at this time of day she would be making her way to

the school canteen to pile her plate high with greasy thick-cut chips and dinosaur-shaped

chicken pieces coated with breadcrumbs. Today, however, she decided to go home for lunch.

She had not seen her grandparents in days, although she knew that they would not have

missed her at all.

She passed through the school gates replaying thoughts of the recent days' events through

her mind. She thought of Mr Darling the milliner; of Judge Cobb and his dog Murphy; of

Isaac, whose bravery had helped to secure Moses' release, and of course, she thought of her

friends the Menzies, whom she would remember always with great love and affection.

Before long she turned into Bott Lane. St Mary Magdalene's Church dominated the view.

Lassa stood at the gateway to the entrance of the churchyard and looked up at the once

magnificent building. It seemed almost inconceivable to think that she had seen the church as

new, with its glorious stained-glass windows and magnificent tower, the stonework of which

was now crumbling, and the plaster render having fallen away long since. Despite having

seen the church hundreds of times before, Lassa noticed for the first time the proud gilded weathercock sitting askew atop the tower, and she wondered if it had been made by Moses

in his smithy.

She felt a lone tear roll down her right cheek as she regarded the boarded up windows,

partly concealed by giant nettles, the deteriorating masonry and the weeds that grew between

the flagstones of the path leading to the church door. It was now a very sorry looking church

indeed.

Lassa pushed at the iron gate and as it creaked open a flock of crows took flight without

warning, and with effortless grace and speed, to flank the long strip of trees down Bott Lane.

She walked down the path towards the church. The sun shone bright and strong across the

catacombs and headstones at either side, causing their shadows to fall back darkly like dominoes, row after row after row. The many statues, much of them vandalised and maimed,

stood lopsided, slumped or face down in mud and bramble.

Lassa did not know what had brought her to the churchyard or indeed what she was

looking for. Until she found it.

At the right side of the path, the first in a row of ten, there stood a plain slab of headstone.

It had sunk into the ground by a good ten inches or more, and up behind it, an angel's arms

rose solemnly, wings folded.

Lassa knelt by the headstone and cleared away the weeds to read the inscription.

In loving memory of Moses Menzies

who died August 28th 1815 aged 90 years.

Beloved husband, devoted father and grandfather

<u>I will lay me down in peace and take my rest</u>

Lassa blew a kiss and tugged one last stubborn weed from the ground. She was glad that he

had died at such a good age.

She shuffled on her knees to look at the next headstone. It too had sunk into the ground by

a good few inches. Moss-covered and worn down with years of hard weather and neglect, the

inscription was almost unreadable. Lassa tore at the long blades of dry grass that had worked

their way between the two stones and brushed away the dust.

<u>In memory of Mary Ann Menzies,</u>

<u>who departed this life on 12th May 1817 aged 87 years.</u>

<u>My body in this earth confined,</u>

<u>Then I four children left behind</u>

T'was pale fac'd Death that brought

me hither,

We liv'd in Love

Let us die together

Gone but not forgotten

Lassa bowed her head and said a small prayer. When she lifted her head moments later, her

eyes were drawn to a pair of gravestones placed back to back slightly off line to the others,

isolated beneath a Yew tree. One had fallen on its side and the nine lines on the epitaph were

almost illegible. But those that Lassa could make out brought gladness to her heart and a

lump to her throat. She had never been so moved. Tears rolled unchecked down her cheeks.

<u>Sacred to the immortal memory of my</u>

<u>dear parents, Jacob John Campion, of this</u>

<u>parish, who departed this life 3rd June 1835</u>

<u>aged 87 years, and Lydia Mary,</u>

<u>who died 1st July 1834 aged 86 years</u>

<u>They were beloved of rich and poor,</u>

<u>Here souls at rest for evermore.</u>

<u>Their devoted daughter,</u>

<u>Lassa</u>

Jacob and Lydia had married! And, what's more, they had named their daughter after her!

Glassy-eyes, Lassa reached around to her back for her rucksack. She removed the flowers

from the outside sleeve and placed them upon the fallen headstone.

"Forget-Me-Nots," she said, echoing Lydia's words and their sentiment. She wiped away

a tear. "Sleep well, Lydia," she whispered.

She rose quietly to her feet and left the churchyard without a backward glance.

*

Lassa was five minutes from home when she encountered Clare Fox, sitting on a garden wall

outside a large semi-detached in Clarke Drive. She was smoking a cigarette and looking

very pleased with herself because of it. Predictably her two cronies, Sam Burdekin and

Michelle Burke, stood before her, chewing on gum, their jaws moving up and down simultaneously like two goldfish in a tank.

Upon seeing her, Clare flicked her cigarette into the kerb and jumped down from the wall.

"Well if it isn't Lardy No-Hope," she sneered.

Lassa stopped dead in her tracks and stared at her unflinchingly. Sam Burdekin and

Michelle Burke drew nearer, still chewing gum and blowing bubbles every other second.

"Surely you're not skipping school lunch today?" Michelle asked, slapping her hands to

her cheeks in mock horror.

"You could probably do with missing a lunch or two," said Clare and Sam and Michelle

cackled like the witches in Macbeth.

Clare prodded Lassa in the belly with a bony finger.

"You're not wrong, Clare," she said. "She's so fat her belly button gets home fifteen

minutes before she does."

Lassa took a deep breath, her scalp tingling in anticipation of what was to come. This was

her first opportunity to prove that she could stand up to her tormentors. <u>If I can survive a</u>

<u>portal into the past, pistol-packing highwayman, leeches, rats and eating enough parsnips to</u>

<u>sink a battleship, then I can survive anything.</u>

"If you must know, I'm going home for my lunch," she told them. She jutted out her chin

defiantly and held Clare's gaze. "Not that it's any of your business," she added boldly.

Clare gave Lassa a dirty look.

"You've got a lot of guts telling me to mind my own business," she said coolly.

Michelle gave a short, nasty laugh. "Oh, she's got a lot of guts for sure!"

Clare approached Lassa until they stood nose to nose.

"Do you want to tell me to mind my own business again?" She grated, her head tilted to

one side, her nostrils flared in anger.

"Why? Are you hard of hearing?" countered Lassa. "Because I don't think I mumbled."

Sam Burdekin and Michelle Burke's mouths fell open in shock, with Michelle losing her

chewing gum to the pavement, taken aback by a side to Lassa she had never seen before.

"You'll pay for that," Clare cautioned menacingly between clenched teeth, her expression

dark.

Lassa held her ground.

"How?" she asked.

With a noise resembling a Viking war cry, Clare took a swing at Lassa. Lassa ducked to

the right, the swing fell wide and Clare's fist made contact with the garden wall with an

ominous-sounding crunch. She cried out in pain and dropped to her knees, cradling her sore

hand in her lap. Sam Burdekin and Michelle Burke rushed to her side, fussing over her.

"I'll be on my way then," Lassa said dispassionately.

She turned on her heel and continued on her way home. She did not look round. Her heart

was beating high, but her cheeks were pale, and as she rounded the corner she leant against a

lamppost and exhaled raggedly. She had done it! She had really done it! No longer would

she be intimidated by Clare Fox. She had stood her ground and had been victorious without

having to raise a hand. It felt good.

She was still smiling to herself three minutes later as she turned the key in the lock of 52a

Dalton House, the small two bedroomed first floor flat she shared with her grandparents.

The door rattled open and seconds later Nance Hope walked into the hall from the kitchen.

She was wiping her hands on her apron.

Without ceremony Lassa ran to her in delight and wrapped her arms around her, kissing her

heartily, and almost throwing her grandmother off balance.

"Hey!" Nance laughed, smiling warmly. "What's brought all this on?" She gave Lassa a

big hug, then held her at arm's length. "It's as though you haven't seen me for a week."

"If only you knew," Lassa thought to herself wryly.

Ern Hope hobbled into the hall, leaning on his walking stick.

Lassa moved away from Nance and rushed over to him. With his free arm, he pulled her close and planted a kiss on top of her head.

"How's my beautiful girl?" he said with great affection.

"Never mind that," Nance said suddenly. A thought had just occurred to her. "What are

you doing home from school at this time of the day?"

Lassa beamed up at them both, her face alive with happiness.

"I just wanted to come home for lunch today," she said.

Her grandfather narrowed his eyes. "You're not avoiding anyone at school, are you?"

Lassa laughed.

"Pops," she said. "I no longer avoid problems, I tackle them head on."

She walked into the living room. Her grandparents looked at each other, but said nothing.

Lassa plonked herself down on the sofa and began to flick idly through the television

channels with the remote control she found lying on its arm.

How she had missed 21st Century technology!

Her grandfather slumped himself down in his favourite armchair and took up his

newspaper.

"Well, Lassa, you chose a good day to come home for lunch," he said.

"Oh yes?" Lassa said cheerily. She felt as though she was the happiest girl in the world,

and that nothing would ever make her frown again. "Why's that then?"

Ern leafed through his broadsheet but he did not look up.

"Your Uncle Bill popped over to gift us some parsnips from his allotment," he told her.

"Your Gran has made some delicious soup from them."

Lassa frowned.

The End

Printed in Great Britain
by Amazon